Ella Hanna

From Stockholm to Salem

Library of Congress Control Number: 2022917920
ISBN: 9798360168683

For my Dad, who helped me bring this story to be

Chapter 1:

"Lana?" I heard a familiar voice call from the distance. It was Salem.

"Looking for the sun? You won't find it here," he called out to me. I laughed. It was dead of night, and I had nowhere else to be. The moon was glistening and peaceful, the way I always remembered it.

"You okay?" He asked, now towering over me. I shrugged. "Here," he said, now extending his hand. I grabbed it and let him pull me out of my trance.

The crickets were chirping. The bushes were rustling from the wind. It had started to rain. Then silence.

Finally, Salem spoke. "Why are you out here, anyway?"

I sighed. "The orphanage is boring. Bland. I'm just not happy here." I grabbed a stick and dragged it around the dirt until it snapped. "But the real question is, why are you out here? I never see you behind the building."

He smirked and unzipped his backpack, revealing a pack of cigarettes. He lit a cigarette using a lighter and inhaled the smoke. I glared at him.

"You're too young for those," I exclaimed, trying to seize the little box. "You're messing up your life early."

He rolled his eyes at my statement. "My life was messed up the day my dad left me here. I've been here for six years, Lana. I have nothing to lose." I could hear the pain in his voice, but he masked it with anger. He puffed the smoke and inhaled again.

I hated seeing him like this, but I knew he was right. What did he care, anyway? He was seventeen, going on eighteen in two weeks. Pretty soon he'd be kicked out onto the streets. And he had no one to support him but me.

He cleared his throat and looked at me. "You know, kid, I'm gonna miss you when I'm out of here. But maybe soon you'll get adopted by someone. Don't ever follow in my footsteps, you hear me?" The rain was starting to pour now, but I didn't care. It was silent and dark inside the orphanage. All the other kids were asleep.

The counselors would kill us if they found us out here, behind the building, especially in the pouring rain. But I'd been out here almost every night, and had never been caught.

I had known Salem for awhile now. Something I had recently picked up on was that he didn't like it when I got too personal. When I initially got here, he was one of the first people who helped me get the hang of things, and I was grateful for that. Since then, we've been inseparable. For someone as simple as he was, he sure had a lot on his mind.

Salem was still smoking his cigarette, but I could tell the rain was starting to annoy him. The crickets that were once chirping had now been quiet. The smell of his cigarette smoke was starting to give me a headache, so I decided to head back inside.

As I entered the corridor, a chill ran up my spine. It was humid outside. Now that I was inside, soaking wet, I was freezing. Careful not to wake anyone, I cautiously stepped into my room.

Phoebe, the girl I shared a room with, was fast asleep. Her blonde hair was tied in a messy pony tail that was now falling apart. She was snoring, but I ignored her and went straight to the closet where I could change into dry clothes to sleep in. It was starting to storm.

I wondered if Salem was still out there. If he was, what was he doing? Anything but smoking, I hoped. I crawled into bed, avoiding the springs.

Phoebe and I were pretty close, but she never advocated for breaking the rules, and couldn't stand when I did. My bed was a metal bed frame with a thin mattress and a few sheets, which was the exact same bed everyone else had.

Phoebe's bed looked like mine, and I'm sure Salem's did, too. Everyone had a pillow, which wasn't luxurious or anything. But by now, I was used to it. Four years was enough - and to think Salem's been here for six.

He never really spoke about why he ended up here, or what his dad was like. All I knew was that his mother was out of the picture. Whether she was dead or alive, I didn't know. And I never bothered to ask.

The next morning came in a blur. Mrs. Diane, an older woman with gray hair and purple glasses, had come into our room and opened the blinds. She did this every morning.

All the kids wake up at eight A.M. to eat breakfast and then got some time to play board games or find something on campus to do. Nothing dangerous was permitted, such as smoking or drinking - everyone knew this. But Salem, being one of the oldest at the orphanage, didn't care about ground rules.

His idea of killing time was smoking cigarettes somewhere in the woods where the counselors couldn't see him. Sometimes I followed him, but I would never touch a cigarette, and I lived by that.

Because there were so many of us, we were hard to keep track of, and as long as we were back by curfew, we weren't sought after. Today was no different. Phoebe and I headed upstairs for breakfast, and I was busy looking for Salem amongst the crowd. I didn't even realize Phoebe was talking to me. I turned to face her. "Sorry, I wasn't paying attention. What did you say?"

Phoebe laughed. "Your hair looks damp. Did you get up early to take a shower?" At first, I had no idea what she was talking about. But then I remembered the rain last night, and having to hurry to bed before anyone noticed me gone. "Yeah," I told her with a smile. She nodded, and that was the end of that conversation.

I immediately noticed Salem already in line for breakfast. I rushed over to him, eager to start my day. When he saw me, his eyes lit up. And mine did, too.

"There you are." I said, flashing him a crooked smile. He smiled back. "If you want anything to eat, you should probably be in line." I shook my head. "I'm not hungry."

After Salem got breakfast, we sat down at a table closest to the back door. He picked at an apple, and after a bit of conversation, Mrs. Diane had announced we could play card games, watch movies, and do whatever we wanted. All the kids shuffled from the tables and into different areas.

Salem threw out the rest of his food and headed for the door, backpack slung over his shoulder. I trailed behind him, trying to keep up with his fast pace.

Just as he opened the back door, Mrs. Diane caught up to us. "You're never inside anymore, Coleman," she nagged. "What are you up to now?"

He brushed the hair out of his face and cleared his throat. "Studying," he told her, and that made her laugh. It was more of a taunting laugh, but he simply just continued out the door and let it shut in her face.

None of the counselors took a liking to Salem, because they always assumed he was up to no good. In reality, he just liked being left alone. It seemed like I was the only exception, and I wasn't really sure why. But I couldn't complain.

After quite a bit of walking, we ended up far away from the building and in a small area secluded by weeds and dead trees. "So," I said. "What are your plans after you turn eighteen?"

He lit a cigarette and shrugged. "I don't know yet. I'll be homeless. Maybe I'll steal cars for a living or something."

I playfully pushed his shoulder. "Don't say that. You have to stay out of trouble. Things will turn around - just wait and see."

He looked at me with those pleading hazel eyes I was really going to miss. "I hope you're right, kid. Maybe getting out of here'll be the best thing that's happened to me in a long time."

Chapter 2:

By now, two weeks had passed. Salem's birthday was today, which meant he was officially an adult.

I made sure to wake up early and head to his room to hand him a letter I'd written the night before. I had a little present for him concealed in a pink sparkly box, so I tucked it underneath my arm along with the letter and quietly hurried over to his room.

I was excited to see his reaction. What would he say? Surely he'd be excited. Maybe even a little emotional. We didn't normally get each other birthday gifts, but this year was different. I might never see him again, so I had to get him a little something. But by the time I got to his room, he was almost done packing his things.

"Already?" I whispered, careful not to wake up the guy sleeping at the other side of his room. "I didn't expect you to leave so early."

He shook his head. "It wasn't my decision. But even if it was, I would've probably left sooner. Lana, please be careful. Maybe I'll see you around someday." He grabbed his stuff and headed for the door.

Without hesitation, I chased after him in the empty hall. "Salem, wait! I have a gift for you."

But he had no time to wait. "Salem?" I called after him. "Lana, please. I have to go." The front door slammed behind him. *Ouch.*

His rush to leave stung a little bit. But regardless of whether or not he planned to say goodbye, he had to have his gift.

I followed after him, and finally, he stopped at a crosswalk. We were now a couple blocks away from the orphanage. This was my chance.

Out of breath, I tugged on his shoulder and he turned to me, startled. "Lana!" He cried. "Are you crazy?"

I handed him the envelope and the tiny box that contained his gift. "Happy Birthday," I gasped. "And now that I've come this far, please let me stay with you."

He took the items and looked at me in disbelief. "You want to - what? Are you serious? Lana, I'm already struggling. You'd be homeless. I can't provide for you. Isn't this illegal? Go back to the orphanage," he sputtered coldly.

I knew he was right. What was I kidding? But seeing the real world so far from the orphanage made me wonder if I could help him out.

Was Mrs. Diane looking for me? I doubted it. What about Phoebe? My belongings? All that was still at the orphanage. But I didn't care anymore.

"I promise we'll be okay," I told him. "Let me help you. Please."

He hesitated. "Lana, you have to go back. Get out of here." His demeanor had darkened.

"Salem, don't be irrational. You know you want to say yes."

He looked at me desperately. "Why would you want to stay with me, anyway? I have nothing. I don't know where to go." By now, the cars had dissipated and he started crossing the street. I followed him.

"I'll help you find a place to stay. I don't want to go back to the orphanage. Just let me stay with you," I pleaded. "What am I gonna do there without you?"

Finally, he gave in. "Alright, kid. Stay with me. But just remember, I'm practically broke and can't really promise you anything." He couldn't hide his smile any longer. I wrapped my arms around him, letting the news sink in. "Thank you."

Salem was looking for a gas station to buy water from, and I was trailing closely behind him, like some lost puppy. We took a turn on a run down street and finally found one.

It was old and had seen better days, but there was still a selection of food and drinks inside. I picked up a case of water and handed it to him.

"That'll be $4.99," said the cashier. She was a young woman wearing red lipstick and hoop earrings. She smiled at me as I dug into my pocket and pulled out some spare change.

Salem covered the rest. He thanked the cashier as he took the water and exited the gas station. I offered to carry it, but he insisted.

"Where to now?" I asked him. He shrugged. "I don't have much money. The options are pretty limited."

I thought for a moment. "We should find a motel," I suggested. He was on board with the idea.

We continued walking for almost an hour before coming across a cheap motel to stay at for the night. Salem used the card given to us by the front desk to get in our room. "212," he said. "Remember that." It was the number of our room.

It was cozy in there, with 2 beds, a little TV, a desk, and some basic kitchen appliances. Salem unpacked his bag and tore open the case of water to grab a bottle. He tossed me one as I sat crisscrossed on the other bed.

"Did you bring anything?" He asked me. I shook my head. "I didn't plan to stay with you, so I left all my stuff at the orphanage."

He looked a little concerned. "We can go back to grab it if you need -" but I stopped him. "Salem, none of my items were important. I'd get into serious trouble if they found out I ran away."

He grimaced. "When you put it that way, it sounds bad. You sure you don't want to go back?"

I shook my head again. "Don't worry about it. I'll be fine. *We'll* be fine," I corrected. I smiled, but he didn't return the favor.

There wasn't much to be done that night. Any money we had before was put towards the motel. I was ready to fall asleep when I saw Salem get out of bed and head out the front door.

"What are you doing?" I asked. But I had my answer when I saw a lighter and a cigarette in his hand. "Seriously?"

"Hey," he said, "you didn't have to come with me. You knew I was going to smoke. I'll be inside in a few." I was a little disappointed, but he had a point. Salem smoking shouldn't have surprised me.

When he got back inside, a feeling of relief rushed through me. I refused to fall asleep until I knew he was safe inside, despite being exhausted.

"Good night," he said to me before turning off a lamp on the desk and climbing into the other bed. It was a lot more comfortable than the bed I was used to at the orphanage. I sank into the mattress and was about to close my eyes before saying, "Good night."

Chapter 3:

When I woke up the next morning, Salem was already outside smoking. It was early. The sun was shining, birds were chirping, and despite this being my first night away from the orphanage, I felt great.

I turned on the TV facing our beds to watch something, but before I could change the channel, I dropped the remote.

"Breaking News," a young male reporter blared. I glanced at the screen.

"Two Norfolk trains have collided in Graniteville. Nine people were killed and roughly more than two hundred people were exposed to toxic chlorine. They are now being treated at a hospital in South Carolina."

Graniteville? That wasn't too far from where we lived. The motel we were at was in North Augusta.

"Hey," said Salem. I jumped. I had no idea he came inside. "Woah," he laughed, "didn't mean to scare you like that. You okay?"

I nodded, then motioned toward the TV.

He shook his head. "Such a shame." He looked sympathetic. My expression darkened, too. It was terrible to think nine people lost their lives when they shouldn't have. What about the other hundreds of people who were exposed to chlorine? I hoped they would make a fast recovery.

I turned the TV off, trying to suffocate the depressive news story. The remote was still on the floor, so I grabbed it and tossed it onto the bed in a state of bewilderment. I had been so out of touch at the orphanage; I forgot things like these still happened everyday.

We didn't have anything to eat in the fridge. I followed Salem to a vending machine not far from our room. We each ate a granola bar and decided to walk around the city.

Surely there had to be cool things to do in South Carolina. We headed out the door of the main entrance and started walking towards cool shops and restaurants.

As we were walking, I observed the other people around us. We were in a crowded area filled with stores and bars. Beside us was a young woman pushing a baby stroller. There was a happy family in the distance sitting near a fountain. Near a bar we had just passed sat a couple I assumed were on a first date.

I looked up at Salem, who was about a foot taller than me. Did he ever get sad the way I did when he saw well-bonded families? Did he ever think there was something more he needed to be happy? I doubted it.

Salem was unreadable. His expression was always blank. He was tough, that was for sure. And defensive. I wondered if it was because of his past or if he just naturally acted that way.

"Hey, Salem?" I asked him. He turned to me and slowed his pace. "Yeah?" I swallowed. "What are the things you need to be happy?"

He frowned. "What do you mean by that?"

I shrugged. "You know. They could be items, or people. Who or what do you need in life to be happy?"

"Me? To be happy? Cigarettes and maybe a credit card. That's all I need to be satisfied."

I waited patiently for him to add, *and you of course.* But when I realized he was finished talking, I looked down at my feet.

Who was I kidding? This was Salem Coleman. The guy who was dumped off at an orphanage by his dad six years ago. The guy who never spoke about his absent mother, or any of his past for that matter. I guess I couldn't expect much of an answer from him. I decided to change the subject.

"Can we get something to eat? I'm starving." We were now sitting on a bench in the lot not far from the crowd.

He nodded. "Sure. But money is a little sparse. We can grab something from the vending machine." He got up from the bench and started walking back the direction we came from. I stood up and followed him.

It felt like we'd been walking for hours. But we were finally almost back to the motel. The vending machine was near the entrance.

I got a sandwich and Salem got a Coke. I looked at the now opened beverage in his hand and tilted my head. "That's all you're eating? Shouldn't you eat more than that?"

He rolled his eyes. "Let me add Coke to my happy list. All I need to be happy is a can of Coke, cigarettes, and a credit card."

I didn't even realize how late it was until I looked around us. The sun was sinking and the sky turned a pinkish orange.

I figured it would be a good idea to head back to our room. When he noticed me walking inside the motel, he followed. I waited for him to insert the key card and then stepped inside.

"I'm gonna take a shower," Salem announced as he threw his backpack onto his bed. He grabbed some clothes and headed to the bathroom.

Exhausted, sore, and now bored, I turned on the TV and fished a water bottle from the case sitting by the mini fridge. Our case of water was starting to diminish.

I yawned and propped my head against the pillow in hopes for a news update about the train disaster I had heard of this morning. But instead, I went numb.

"A local teenager has been deemed missing as of six A.M. on Saturday," a news reporter explained. "It is known she had been living in an orphanage and was last seen Friday night. She is sixteen years old and does not have a vehicle."

The reporter continued my description. "If you or someone you know have any details regarding her disappearance, please contact the North Augusta police department. The young girl's name is Lana Garcia, and she does not have any complicated medical history."

A picture of me appeared on the screen before the channel shifted to another news story. And in a flash, reality hit me that someone noticed me gone and wanted me back.

Chapter 4:

My heart was beating rapidly. I turned off the TV in a panic. How had they noticed me gone?

It hasn't been that long, and there were so many kids in the building. Then I remembered - Phoebe.

I couldn't say I hated Phoebe, considering we were friends, and had been living in the same room together for years. Besides, she probably alerted counselors in hopes of bringing me back. But if she had known I didn't want to return, would she still have told someone?

My head was spinning. Knowing they had my info and were now searching for me made me surge with anger. I hated the orphanage, and I'd do anything to avoid it. I thought I'd made it pretty obvious I wanted to be forgotten.

By now, Salem was out of the shower and dressed in sweatpants and a loose T-shirt. He must've noticed the concern on my face, because he hurriedly rushed over to me and asked what was wrong.

"I'm fine," I told him. My voice was shaky, and I was hoping he didn't notice. "Don't worry." He went to sit on his bed, but I could still feel his eyes on me.

How was I going to tell him? I was worried if I told him, he'd panic and make me go back. Salem was legally an adult now, and the orphanage knew he had moved out. But me on the other hand? I was sixteen and still their responsibility.

Salem didn't have the cleanest reputation, but harboring a minor wasn't something even he'd want on his record.

I didn't want Salem to worry about me. What if he called police and told them I was with him? I couldn't tell him. He was already reluctant with the idea of letting me into his life. But how was I going to keep this from him? Our city wasn't very big, and kids, let alone orphans, didn't disappear out of the blue.

Eventually, Salem fell asleep. I was laying in my bed, tossing and turning. There was no chance I'd sleep tonight.

My head throbbed and my mind was still racing. This was one of the many times I'd wished my brain had an off switch.

I looked at the time on the clock above the TV. It was eleven minutes past twelve. Midnight, and I was still wide awake.

I got up from my bed and stepped out the door. What was I doing? I had no idea. I just needed fresh air. I peered inside the room making sure Salem was still asleep and cautiously shut the door. Then I proceeded to walk through the main entrance.

It was now colder outside. I was in a tank top and shorts. The woman working at the front desk was typing something on the computer. "You okay, dear?" She asked me as I made my way to the front door. I looked at her and nodded.

"Where's your boyfriend?" I froze. Then started to laugh. "Salem? He's not my boyfriend. We're -" I paused. "Friends." I wanted to say best friends, but I wasn't sure if Salem considered me his best friend. We were good friends, and it worked well that way.

I was sitting on an old, rusty bench outside the motel. South Carolina was pretty at night. I guess anywhere but the orphanage was pretty in my eyes. I looked up at the stars and thought of Phoebe.

I don't know why Phoebe came to mind when I saw the stars, but I was still focused on earlier. Was she sad I was gone? Did she miss me?

I guess I had never really considered her feelings. Maybe she would've liked to run away with me. I felt guilty. I hoped she wasn't worried. Did she think I was kidnapped? Or worse - dead?

A chill ran through my spine. One problem at a time. I didn't need any more stress.

It was getting colder now, and I decided to head back inside. The woman at the front desk didn't acknowledge me as I walked past her and down the hall.

I read each of the room numbers - 209, 210, 211 - 212. The door wasn't completely shut. I had left it that way so I could easily get back in without the card.

Salem was still passed out. He was submerged under the covers. His dark, wet hair was all I could see.

I climbed into my own bed. But even after my short, peaceful encounter with the stars and cold weather, I couldn't bear going to sleep. My eyes wouldn't close.

I still felt guilty. Guilty for leaving Phoebe without any notice. Guilty for not telling Salem I was deemed as missing. How long would it take for police to start searching for me? It had only been a few hours since my picture appeared on the news. Would they even bother searching for someone who wasn't tied to a family?

I somehow managed to stay up the whole night. I was sleep deprived. The sun was finally here.

Salem was still asleep. I stood up and walked to the bathroom mirror to see my reflection. There were now bags under my eyes.

I turned the TV back on and adjusted the volume to the lowest setting so I didn't wake Salem. Anything to take my mind off things. But it didn't take long for him to wake up.

"Lana?" He said groggily. "Why are you up so early?"

I shrugged. "Sorry if I woke you up. I'm just a little bored. So I'm watching TV." He glanced at the clock and yawned. "It's six in the morning. Shouldn't you go back to sleep?" *If only he knew*, I thought. There was no going back to sleep. There was no sleep to begin with.

"Can we go on a walk?" I blurted. I wanted to be outside. Not out in the open, but at least in the sun.

"Lana. Are you not aware it's six A.M.?" He growled. "I'm tired." Unlike me, Salem was not a morning person. I was never up this early, but I was wide awake despite running on no sleep.

After he noticed my face drop in disappointment, he climbed out of bed and slid on his shoes.

"Wait, you're coming on a walk with me?" My eyes lit up with excitement. He rolled his eyes, but smiled. "Sure. If you really wanna take a walk, let's go for it." He grabbed his backpack and headed out the door without saying another word.

We had just left the motel and were now on a road filled with gravel and dirt. The sun was just starting to rise. The road we were on finally took us to the main street with the most attraction, and even that area was almost empty this early.

As we were walking, I noticed a large wall plastered on the side of a building with shops. There were all sorts of papers, flyers, and posters overlapping each other on the wall. But the one that stood out to me the most was a white poster neatly typed - with my picture on it.

Seriously? It had the word "Missing" printed on the top in bold letters. So they were out for me.

It looked as if it had been freshly stapled on the board. There were a small handful of "Missing" posters close to mine, but most of them looked like they'd been sitting here for years. The rest of the papers were all worn and tearing, while my poster was the newest addition.

"You know," Salem said, "I used to walk around these roads all the time. My dad used to take me to all sorts of forbidden areas when we had nothing better to do."

"Oh, really?" I said, still studying the poster. "That sounds like fun." I didn't want Salem to see the poster, and know I was missing. Or anyone, for that matter.

"Yeah. I sure do miss the old man sometimes." I nodded to him, now trying to slowly tear the poster from the bulletin board. Each of the corners were stapled. I managed to get one corner loose, and then another.

"Maybe it wasn't such a bad idea to come out here after all. The sun is pretty when it's not blinding you."

I was trying to focus on what he was saying while tearing off the poster. "You're right," I said, trying to sound attentive. "See? It's nice out here in the open." Another corner was retrieved from the board.

It was so relieving when I carefully managed to pull the last corner off the board. Now that the poster was in my hand, I crumpled it up and shoved it into the pocket of my jeans.

Salem was still admiring the sun, and his back was turned to me. Now that the poster was in my pocket, I took his hand and led him away from the bulletin board.

"Where are we going?" He asked with surprise. To be honest, I didn't know where we were going. Anywhere but the main street. As more people started arriving, I grew frantic. I pulled him into a small pizzeria that had just opened. He laughed.

"Are you hungry?" I shook my head. "It was getting hot outside." I bit my lip and hoped he wouldn't correct me, because it was actually windy outside. He didn't.

By now, workers behind the counter had seen us. "Welcome!" Said a man in a chef's apron. "How can I help you?"

I didn't want to seem out of place. "Two lemonades please," I said. Salem glared at me. "I don't like lemonade." It was my turn to roll my eyes. "More for me then."

The worker smiled and grabbed two glasses for our drinks. I watched as he scooped some ice out of a cooler, filled the glasses with freshly squeezed lemonade, and grabbed two straws.

"Here," said the man. "$1.97 is your total." I wasn't even thirsty, but I still grabbed the drinks. Salem seized some cash and handed it to the man. He took back the change and stuffed it in his pocket. I grabbed the straws and we headed out the door.

"It was hotter in there than outside," he grumbled. "Now that you have your lemonade, can we find something else to do?" I took a sip and followed him as he started walking. "Of course."

We were starting to run out of ideas on where to go. Were we going to live this free lifestyle forever? It seemed like it. "We can go to the pool if you want," said Salem. "It's free."

I liked this idea, given that it was a Monday and there probably wouldn't be too many people. "But I don't have a bathing suit."

He thought for a moment. "Right. I forgot you left almost all your stuff behind. Would you mind wearing a shirt and shorts? I probably have something you can wear."

I couldn't tell if he was being serious, but judging by his facial expression, he wasn't kidding. "Sure," I said. His clothes were probably bigger than mine, but that worked out. Anything loose and comfortable.

We walked back to the motel. Salem inserted the card, opened the door, and dug in the dresser by his bed. He pulled out a shirt with the word "Rochester" printed on the front.

"What's that?" I asked Salem as he tossed the shirt onto his bed. He looked at me. "What's what?" I pointed to the shirt. "What's Rochester?"

He laughed. "It's a city in New York. I was born there." I was surprised. All this time I had thought Salem lived in South Carolina since he was born. I hadn't ever taken into consideration just how private he really was.

"When did you move here?" I asked him. He was now digging in another drawer for shorts. "We moved here when I was ten. I was dumped at the orphanage when I was twelve."

I nodded. It took me everything to keep my mouth shut. I wanted to ask so many more questions about his early life. But I didn't. I grabbed the clothes he handed me and changed in the bathroom.

The shirt was really big on me, but I tucked it into the shorts so it didn't look weird. I studied myself in the mirror. The bags under my eyes were still very much visible from my lack of sleep. Did he notice them? Maybe he didn't want to ask about them. I didn't blame him.

I didn't look the most flattering in Salem's oversized shirt and baggy shorts, but it was manageable. We started walking to the pool, which, according to Salem, was nearby. It was a long walk. My worn sandals were hurting my feet.

When we finally saw the large community pool in the distance, a wave of relief rushed over me. As we grew closer, I realized there were a lot more people on a Monday than I expected.

I took a deep breath. *No one will notice*, I told myself. I stepped into the now open pool gate and hoped no one in this small city recognized me as Lana Garcia, the sixteen year old missing girl who had no vehicle, and no complicated medical history, according to the news. The girl who ran away from the orphanage just a mere two days ago.

Without hesitation, I jumped into the pool. There were kids splashing each other, and parents sun tanning in pool chairs. Everyone seemed to be having a good time.

The shirt I was wearing started to weigh down with water, and so did the shorts. I climbed out of the pool and waited for Salem to get in, ringing out my shirt. He jumped and laughed as I scurried after him.

We received disapproving looks as we splashed each other with water, but I didn't pay attention. I guess teenagers having fun in the pool was unheard of or something.

I was having a good time. A great time. I couldn't remember the last time I swam in a pool. Just letting the water touch my skin was enough to make me want to stay forever. My hair was soaked. Salem was close behind me. I assumed he was enjoying the water too. A genuine smile spread across his face; one I hadn't seen before.

He always looked miserable at the orphanage, but almost everybody did. Leading my own life, making my own decisions, and exploring the city of North Augusta at my own pace was so rewarding. I didn't need fancy materials to be satisfied. Or any for that matter. I thought back to the bag of items still sitting somewhere in my room. I guess I wasn't getting those back, but I didn't really miss them anyway.

Salem and I were still swimming in the pool. Two other kids were playing with each other a few feet from us.

A man with blonde hair who looked to be in his twenties was sitting on a chair while fiddling with his flip phone. He was staring at me intently.

He had a distinct yellow canary tattoo plastered on his neck that made him stand out like a sore thumb. I didn't want to make eye contact with him, but I could feel his stare from the corner of my eye. Why was he staring at me?

I guess Salem noticed this too, because after a few minutes had passed, he was now staring back at the guy. "Need something?" Salem said in a now slightly irritated tone.

I tugged Salem's arm in hopes to get him away from the guy. The man fell out of his intent gaze. "No sir," he said. "It's just - you -" he was now pointing at me.

Alarms were going off in my head. I knew the only way he recognized me was from the news. I tugged Salem's arm again, this time harder, but he gently pushed me away. "What about her?"

Now I was panicking. "Salem, let's go," I hissed. The man was studying my face.

I didn't want him to say anything about me. What if he reported me to the police? "Salem, let's go," I repeated through gritted teeth. "Let's not bother this gentleman." I plastered a fake smile on my face.

Salem was surely the defensive type. But I didn't think he could get defensive of other people. All this time I had thought he was just selfish. Was he defending me?

To my relief, Salem finally stepped out of the pool and followed me to the pool gate, where I had been standing. Was the man still staring at me? I didn't care. I was too scared to turn around.

I continued my pace with Salem, and the two of us were now on some road further away from the pool. He had been silent, but then he broke the tension. "Did you know that guy?" He asked me.

I shook my head. I wasn't lying about that part. I had never seen him in my life. But I knew *why* he was staring at me. At least, I was pretty positive.

"I'm sorry," Salem muttered. "Too much?" I didn't answer. Eventually, Salem turned to me again. "Do you have any idea what he was talking about?"

I shook my head again. I felt too guilty to speak real words. "Are you mad at me?" He asked.

I blinked. "Of course not. Why would I be?" I was trying to sound sincere, but it was hard as I was admittedly a little annoyed.

"Well, I kind of blew our trip to the pool. I didn't mean to cause a scene. I wanted to know what his problem was." He kicked the rocks on the road we were still walking on.

I felt bad he was taking the blame for this whole thing when it was actually my fault. I shouldn't have ran away with him. People were looking for me.

That man wasn't delusional. He thought I was the girl from the news. And he was right.

He probably just wanted the best for me. To return me home.

Only I didn't have a home. The closest thing to my home was room 212 in some run down motel I'd only been staying at for a few days. But it still somehow felt more comfortable than the cold, small room I shared with Phoebe back at the orphanage. Before I knew it, my eyes started to water.

"Lana?" Salem stopped walking and put his hand on my shoulder. "What's wrong? Did you get hurt?"

I couldn't talk through the tears. I needed space. I pushed him aside and continued walking. "Lana!" He called out. He tried running after me, but I ignored him. "I'm sorry," I muttered as I turned into a dark alleyway. I hoped I had lost him.

I needed to clear my thoughts. My head was spinning again. I buried my face in my knees and sobbed. I didn't care if someone noticed me then. I just needed some time to reflect.

I woke up and took a deep breath. It took me a second to remember why I was passed out in an alleyway far from the motel. Right. I was crying. But now I was freezing. I was still soaked from my trip to the pool. In Salem's clothes.

Salem. Was he mad? Worried? I stood up, brushed myself off, and hurried out of the darkness. It was a little brighter in the open, but darker than I remembered. How long had I been asleep? It was just then that I realized I was lost. Without Salem, I had no idea where to go.

There was a gas station nearby. I recognized it as the same gas station Salem and I stopped at to get water almost a week ago. I finally accepted the fact that I needed directions.

It was a big risk walking into that gas station knowing anyone could see me, but I had no other option.

"Hey honey," Said a middle-aged woman wearing heavy makeup. She smiled at me as I stepped towards the front counter. This woman was new. I hadn't seen her here before.

"Hi," I said, trying not to shiver. "Do you know where the nearest motel is?" I was stupid. I didn't even know the name of the motel we were staying at. But there weren't too many around here. I was hoping she'd direct me to the right one.

She thought for a moment and then smiled. "There's one a few miles from here," she said. "It's pretty run down, but it's not too far away." That was definitely the one. It was the cheapest motel around here.

"Anyway, you walk down the road, take a right after a few miles, and walk straight. It should be there." I thanked her and forced a smile.

I felt sick. But I hurried out of the gas station and started back to the motel in Salem's wet Rochester shirt and gym shorts.

Here I was, standing in front of room 212. I was hesitant. I knew I had to knock at some point, but this was bound to be awkward. I built up the courage and gently knocked. This was going to be hard. But he'd come around eventually, right?

After a few seconds, he opened the door. "Lana?" He said. The stress on his face melted into relief. But then he clenched his fists. "Where were you?" He demanded.

I swallowed. "I - had a little breakdown." He rubbed at his forehead and turned away from me. "Oh. I get it." I was more than happy to hear he understood. "You threw a tantrum and ran away, because that's the best way to get rid of your problems, isn't it?" He raved.

My heart raced. "No, Salem, it's not like that - "

"It's not?" He protested. "I'm starting to think you coming with me was a bad idea. You're causing me worry. Wasn't that exactly what you said you wouldn't do?"

"Look, I needed time to myself, to reevaluate everything, and -"

"Reality check. It's just you and me now. Nobody else. If the two of us don't stick together, we'll be alone. And I'd do fine by myself, but I don't think you would. Do you know how dangerous that is?"

I couldn't look him in the eyes. "I'm going through a lot right now. Give me a break."

He scoffed. "I know you're younger than me, but life doesn't care about how young you are. If you don't start toughening up now, you and I are gonna be stuck in this little motel forever. Or maybe on the bench outside of it if we're lucky."

He waited for me to respond, but it was hard to when he was drilling me with so much shit. All I could say was, "I'm pretty sure we're just damn unlucky."

"*Unlucky*? We have a roof over our heads. Well, for now. You know, I'm not gonna try to change your thinking process or whatever, but I hope you realize things could be way worse."

He grabbed a cigarette and shoved past me, this time not so gently. I didn't try to stop him.

But not before telling me, "So Lana, you better start counting our blessings, cause we don't have very many."

Chapter 5:

That was a week ago.

I hated to admit it, but Salem was right about what he said back in the motel. About counting our blessings. And so I did start counting them, just to see what would happen.

I realized after tallying them up that he was right about the last part, too - we didn't have very many. But we had *enough*.

Now, we were closer than ever. And I'd be lying if I didn't tell you we were leaving North Augusta.

It was my idea. I didn't want people to find me. I liked being with Salem. It was difficult convincing him to leave the city, and I could see why. The two of us had memories here. I was born here.

Salem had grown attached to the city ever since he moved from Rochester. But I knew it was too risky to stay. If anyone saw me, I'd be back at the orphanage in a heartbeat. Only this time, without Salem. And more restrictions.

As I started cleaning out the motel room, Salem was reading about cities we could potentially live in. "Greenwood," he said. "Greenwood, South Carolina." Without questioning, I nodded. "Pack your stuff."

And just like that, we were on a train to Greenwood, South Carolina. Salem checked out of room 212 and we finally managed to find a train station. When the train finally came, a knot formed in my stomach. Was this the right choice?

Salem ushered me into the train as he followed closely behind me. No turning back now. Was Greenwood, South Carolina the right place to stay? What would we do? I'd never even seen this part of South Carolina.

Salem and I found seats in the back of the train. It was dark outside. We had been pondering this decision all day.

"You really want to leave your hometown?" Salem said just as I was about to fall asleep in my seat. "Yeah." He paused in thought. "Why?"

I couldn't tell him the real reason why. "Bad memories at the orphanage, that's all. Besides, don't you think it got boring after a while? I want a fresh start." Part of this was true. But it wasn't my genuine reason. He didn't question me after that.

By the time we reached Greenwood, it was even darker. Salem tapped me on the shoulder after the train halted. As people started piling off the train, the two of us started gathering our bags. There wasn't much to carry because we packed so lightly. I hardly had anything to bring.

After everyone had shuffled out of the train, we stood up and walked down the aisle. This was it. Greenwood, South Carolina.

It was a small city, and there wasn't much to see in the dead of night. But I knew when morning came there'd be much more to explore.

As we walked down the street, I grabbed a newspaper from a tourist stand waiting by the train station. *Woman, 19, Found Dead In Her Greenwood Home* was the title. I showed Salem the newspaper.

"Can you believe this?" I continued reading. *Felicia White, age 19, was found dead in her home last week. Police have yet to find the person behind the cold-blooded murder.*

This was alarming to say the least. "Great. We move into a city where a murder has just been committed," I muttered. I was starting to regret the decision of leaving North Augusta already.

"Lana, relax. That had to have been a coincidence. I'm sure whoever did it will be found tomorrow and put behind bars for life." Maybe he was right. With Salem by my side, I was practically untouchable. I just hoped Felicia would get her justice.

After noticing Salem yawn, I could tell he was just as tired as I was. "I guess this is the part where we find a motel?" He said, staring off into the distance.

I didn't even really think about that. I was too worked up in the newspaper article that I forgot we were still standing by a train station in a new city. "Right. But I don't think we can walk to a motel. How will we get there?"

Chapter 6:

Never in a million years did I think I would hitchhike. But here we were, late at night, standing by the edge of a run down street.

"Seriously?" I asked Salem as he stuck his thumb out facing the road. It took me everything to hold my laugh in. "Couldn't we have just taken a cab or something?"

He laughed. "That's boring. And we'd have to leave a tip."

I groaned. "You really think someone's going to pick us up on a road like this?" For the record, there were no cars in sight.

"Chill out, kid. Someone has to turn up at some point." I hoped he was right. I was about to curl up at the side of the road and doze off again like I did on the train. But surprisingly after twenty minutes, a shiny black Porsche slowed down as it neared us. As soon as the car stopped, Salem put his thumb down and grabbed his bag. I did the same.

"You sure this is a good idea?" I muttered. But before he could answer, the driver started to roll down his window. "Need a ride?" The driver asked, who was now revealed to be a middle aged man with a husky beard and beady silver eyes.

Saying this man looked sketchy would be an understatement. I was terrified, but Salem took my hand and led me into the backseat.

"What are two teens like you doing out here alone, anyway?" Said the man.

"We're orphans," I mumbled. "We just moved here." The man grunted heavily and continued focusing on the road. It took me a few minutes to realize that he didn't even ask us where we needed to go.

"Um, sir?" I asked him wearily. "Could you take us to the nearest motel?" No answer. After exchanging a worried glance with Salem, he spoke up. "Sir, it's getting late. We need to find a motel."

The man sighed. "I had a son," he began. "A brilliant minded son. He died a few years ago."

Now he was staring at us through the rearview mirror. "I'm sorry," I said, unsure of what to say. I cringed.

"No," he said. "It wasn't your fault. It's just-" he trailed off for a moment. "You kids remind me of him. Do you need a place to stay?"

I felt bad for the man, but my instincts told me his offer was a little too broad for a yes or no. For this, I remained silent.

"Yes," Salem blurted. "We would love a place to stay." I shot him a dirty look. What was he thinking?

The man grinned. "Great! I live in a beautiful house just down the street. Stay as long as you need. There's an extra bedroom upstairs."

Why was he so excited? Did he need company? If that was the case, we were not the right kind of company for a middle-aged man like him.

"I'm Trevor, by the way," he said. "And you guys are?"

I didn't want to give him my name. But after Salem did, I felt obliged to. "Lana," I said. The whole rest of the ride was silent. And it was awfully long for a house that was supposedly "just down the street".

We pulled into the driveway of a beautiful house. My jaw dropped when I saw it for the first time. It practically screamed privilege and luxury. I could tell Salem was now having second thoughts about the whole thing.

"Gather your bags," Trevor said. "Here it is." As Trevor began heading to the front door, I grabbed Salem's hand. "What the hell are you doing?" I exclaimed. "We can't just move into a stranger's house."

He rolled his eyes. "This is a huge mansion. What's better than living rent-free in a house that probably has diamond-plated countertops?" His eyes were practically glowing as he admired the property in front of us.

He had a point. I guess this was far better than paying a fortune of our small sliver of money left for a dirty motel room. And what would happen once we ran out of money? I thought back to our now empty case of water back at the motel. "I'm coming," I yelled as I grabbed my things and headed for the porch.

As soon as the door swung open, I was hit in the face with a clean, rich smell. I couldn't put my finger on what the smell was; it just smelled rich. I was in awe as I stared at the beautiful paintings and leather furniture.

"Salem and Lana," Trevor said. "Here's a room you two can share. This was my son, Hudson's room. That was his name." He gushed while standing in the doorway. "Just don't touch anything, okay?" Then he walked off.

"I didn't know we'd be staying in his dead son's room," Salem whispered. I could tell he felt uneasy. "Me neither."

As Salem started brushing his teeth, I took it upon myself to explore the room. The walls were a dark cobalt blue. There was a closet in the corner of the room, but it was boarded up with thin planks of wood. A painting was above the king-sized bed. In the painting were trees surrounding a lake. The painted forest was dark, just like the rest of the room. Even the bedsheets were a dark, lifeless gray.

There was a window, but thick, velvet curtains prevented me from seeing the outside. I paced around the room slowly, glancing at every little artifact that now preserved Hudson's existence. There was a black dresser with a football on it. Several picture frames were neatly arranged on this dresser. They were covered in dust, but also clear enough to see the photos. One picture had a teenage boy in it with dusty blonde hair that looked more like a light brown, who I assumed was Hudson. The other was a picture of Trevor and Hudson together. Trevor was smiling as Hudson held a sparkler up to the camera.

The last photo was a clear image of Trevor and a woman hugging each other. The woman had a striking resemblance to Hudson, so it must've been his mother. Where was she, anyway? From what I knew, Trevor lived alone in this breath-taking palace.

"This is awesome, right Lana?" Salem asked me as I climbed into bed. "Yeah," I said. "It's pretty nice." I was positive he could tell I was lying through my teeth. After all, I was still pretty weary of staying in a stranger's house, regardless of their net worth.

I could hear Salem tossing and turning on his side of the bed. I didn't blame him. The bed was pretty uncomfortable from remaining untouched for so long. It was one in the morning.

"Lana?" said Salem. "Yes?"

He paused for a minute. "Remember that night in the rain?" It took me a second to understand what he was talking about. But I nodded.

"It was pouring down rain, and we just sat there. Had a long conversation. I was smoking and you were okay with it. I appreciate you, kid. I mean it."

I smiled. His words meant a lot to me. Someone who looked so heartless and cold at the orphanage was now telling me how much he appreciated me. That had to be worth something. Even half asleep, I knew this.

"I appreciate you, too," I said with drowsiness in my voice. Because of how drained I was, it wasn't hard to fall asleep fast. Within a few minutes, I had passed out. "Goodnight Salem," I said. But he was already asleep.

Chapter 7:

"Salem?" I called out as I stepped outside the room. The clock read 1:32 P.M. How had I slept this late?

From the looks of it, he was already awake. As I made my way to the living room of Trevor's beautiful house, I saw Salem watching football on the huge flat screen TV. "Lana! Good morning," he said, eyes still glued to the TV.

"Good morning," I smiled. Seeing him so amped made me feel happier. There weren't really any TVs at the orphanage, so he probably didn't get to do this often.

"Hey." I turned my head to see Trevor, who was now in the kitchen. "Hi Trevor," I said. I still didn't fully trust him. He was still a stranger, after all.

But Salem didn't seem alarmed. He lounged on the sofa as if he didn't have a care in the world. Maybe I was overreacting. This man was probably just a kind father still grieving over the loss of his son, and maybe having us over filled some sort of empty void in his heart.

"There's a whole shelf of books in the living room if you like to read," said Trevor, now pointing to a tall bookshelf. I nodded and walked over to it.

Seeing so many books reminded me of the orphanage. There were lots of books in the common area that us kids liked to read. My favorite book was always "Ulysses" by James Joyce. Phoebe and I would always read it together.

Phoebe. I had completely forgotten about her. What was she doing now? Did she miss me? I felt guilty that I had left her behind. But it was for the best. It wasn't like she knew Salem anyway. I shook the orphanage thoughts and steered my attention towards the bookshelf now towering over me.

There were lots of classic novels, including "The Great Gatsby", "Jane Eyre", "The Call of the Wild", and "Moby Dick". After skimming through all the options, I settled on a book called "Beloved" by Toni Morrison.

"What book are you reading?" Asked Salem. I held up the classic novel to show him. "It's called Beloved."

A few chapters in, I started growing bored of reading. As I set down the book, I noticed Trevor from the corner of my eye stacking what looked to be newspaper clippings. As he shuffled them all in a neat pile, he frantically shoved them into a drawer in the kitchen. Maybe he collected newspapers? I brushed the idea off and sat next to Salem on the sofa.

"Still watching TV?" I laughed. He snapped back to reality and glanced over at me. "Sorry," he said. He finally turned off the TV and stood up. "Wanna go somewhere?"

I thought about it for a moment and agreed. It felt nice knowing we were living rent-free in a safe environment. Or at least, it seemed safe enough. Since we now had extra money on our hands, we were free to spend some of it, right?

"You kids going somewhere?" Asked Trevor as I slid on my sandals. "Yeah," I said. "We'll be back later tonight." He laughed. "Don't worry about the time. Just stay safe. Do you need to borrow my car?"

His question took me by surprise. I looked at Salem and he grinned. I could tell he was gonna have fun with this opportunity.

"Yes sir, if you don't mind," he said. Salem had his driver's license, even though he didn't have a car. I on the other hand, did not. Despite recently turning sixteen, I had yet to take my Driver's Test. But that could wait. It's not like I needed one, anyway. I didn't own a car either. But when I watched as Trevor handed his car keys to Salem, I was thrilled. We had so much power with the use of a car. An expensive one. No more walking on foot.

"Thank you," I said to Trevor. It felt like we won the jackpot. We had access to a shelter, food, and a car, all for free. I had my doubts when we first crossed paths with Trevor, but it must've been fate or something. All my worried thoughts faded as I climbed into the back of his beautiful black Porsche. The car was clean and smelled new.

"Where to?" Asked Salem as he got behind the wheel. He turned the key in the ignition and started up the car.

We sat in the car for a long time, reflecting on possible ideas. As my eyes darted around the gorgeous interior of the car, Salem's face lit up.

"Arcade!" he exclaimed with excitement. "I haven't been to one in forever." I shot him a confused look. "What's that?"

His mouth dropped as soon as I spoke. "You haven't been to an arcade? Not once?"

I shook my head. I wasn't an orphan for as long as Salem was, but there were still a lot of cool things I'd never done before. I guess this was one to add to the list. But it didn't stay there for long, because Salem put the car in drive and sped down the road.

"We are so going to an arcade," he said. "I can't believe you've never been to one."

From how shocked he was, I couldn't believe it either. Before my life as an orphan, I spent all my time with my grandmother. My real mother didn't want me in her life, and my father was out of the picture.

I had done a lot of things with my grandma before her sudden death. Maybe I really had been to an arcade when I was little, but I surely didn't remember. All my thoughts were interrupted when we pulled up to an extravagant building with flashing lights inside. "We're here," said Salem. "Come on."

I followed him into the arcade, unsure of what to expect. My eyes instantly widened as I saw how magical this place was. There were arcade machines everywhere, toy cranes, upbeat music blasting, and wildly colored lights surrounding the place.

I was so used to a boring life at the orphanage by now. To an average kid with a normal life, this place might've just been a cool spot to go to every once in a while. But to me, this place was amazing. Little kids ran screaming around all the arcade games as Salem was exchanging our cash for quarters. When he finished, he handed me a stack of the coins and told me to go do whatever I wanted with them.

Without hesitation, I ran over to the nearest machine I could find and shoved a handful of quarters into the coin slot. Salem went next door to the gas station where he could buy a pack of cigarettes before joining me. I was too mesmerized by the arcade game in front of me to even be mad.

After finishing the first game, I headed over to the next. My plan was to play as many different games as I could with the amount of quarters I had. After gathering my tickets, I went to another arcade game. And then another.

"Having fun?" I was playing my fourth arcade game that night. "Hey Salem," I beamed. I showed him all the tickets I had won so far.

"Awesome!" He said, now pulling out the quarters from his pocket. "Want to race?"

He motioned over to a racing game with sports cars. I had never played it before, so of course I followed him.

I climbed onto the fake yellow car and he took the red one next to me. I pushed my quarters through the slot and waited for him to do the same.

"Ready?" He asked as he finished entering the last coin. I nodded with a bold smile. "Ready."

There were so many fun games we had played so far. Salem went to get more quarters and I began playing another arcade game next to the front counter.

"Here," he said, now holding another handful. I grabbed half of the quarters and raced to a machine when Salem stopped me. "Want to push our luck?" He laughed. He was now pointing to a large toy crane filled with stuffed animals of all colors and sizes. I went over to the crane and put in 4 quarters.

"I'm not good at these," I grumbled as I fiddled with the lever. I stopped the claw above a huge teddy bear sitting in the middle of the machine. I crossed my fingers and watched as the claw lowered, but no such luck. I could hear Salem snickering as I watched in disappointment, but then he shoved me aside and took the lever. "Let me show you how it's done."

I watched in amazement as the claw, positioned just right above the huge brown teddy, grasped onto it and dropped it through the winner slot.

"Impressive," I sneered. But what I didn't expect was for him to pull the teddy bear out of the slot and hand it to me.

"You're giving this to me?" I asked.

He nodded. "It's for you," he said. "Are you sure?" He rolled his eyes. "It's not like I just gave you a hundred dollars," he said. "The bear is yours. Besides, what am I gonna do with it?"

A huge smile spread across my face. Surely Salem didn't think much of his little token, but giving me this teddy bear made me feel so special. "Thank you," I said. "I love it."

I held on tight to the teddy bear and continued playing fun games with Salem as the night progressed. After finally running out of quarters, we decided it was time to head back to Trevor's before I spent all our money.

But before we collected our prizes and gathered our things, I couldn't help but notice the guy with the blonde hair from the pool standing on the other side of the building. *What the hell?*

Was he following us or something?

After staring at him for awhile, I decided telling Salem would ruin our fun night. It's not like he was looking at us or anything. It must've been some creepy coincidence. So I brushed it off.

"Do you think Trevor will be mad at us for returning his car so late?" I asked as we left the arcade.

He shook his head. "Of course not. We weren't out for that long. Man, I have to start conditioning you for actual late nights."

I folded my arms. "What's that supposed to mean?"

"It means you're too soft," he said. "When we go to a party, you really need to get used to this."

I glanced at the time. It was eleven o'clock.

Still clutching my new teddy bear, I took a seat in the car and put on my seatbelt. "You really like that bear, huh?" I heard Salem say as I positioned it in front of me.

"Of course," I said. "It was a really sweet gift." Salem started up the car and pulled out of the parking lot.

It didn't take long for us to arrive at Trevor's extravagant house. The beautiful mansion staring up at me made me feel comfortable. Like I belonged here. Like I was finally living the life I had always dreamed of living. I took a deep breath and rang the doorbell.

Trevor answered the door and let us in. "Did you kids have fun?" He asked with a bright, almost fake, smile. I nodded.

Salem trailed inside after me and handed Trevor his car keys. "Thanks for letting us use your car," he said. Trevor laughed. "Anytime."

I went upstairs and changed into loose clothes. Just as I went into Hudson's bathroom to brush my teeth, I realized I was starving. I didn't really eat anything today because I was so distracted from our fun day at the arcade. The happy high I was facing was enough to keep me full for the whole day.

I went downstairs to the kitchen where I saw Salem and Trevor having a conversation. "Hey Lana," said Salem. "Did you know this guy is a psychiatrist?"

He was now pointing to Trevor with amazement. "Really?" I said as I reached for a banana on the table. "Is that why you have so much money?"

Trevor nodded. "I work a lot to support myself. I was also born into a rich family. A lot of the money I own was inherited." I peeled the banana and took a bite as I continued listening to Trevor and Salem.

"So, you're insanely rich?" Asked Salem as he admired the mansion around him. Trevor grinned. "You could put it that way."

Salem wasn't wrong. This guy was stupid rich. The chances of one of the richest people in this city taking us in as orphans I concluded to be pure luck. Maybe everything was meant to be this way. I sighed a happy sigh and went back upstairs.

As soon as I reached my bed, I collapsed onto it and hugged my big teddy bear. I felt so secure in this house. Under these covers. This had to be fate. My new, rich lifestyle was amazing. What was I worried about again?

Chapter 8:

"Pass me the sunscreen," I said to Salem as I slid on my sunglasses. Another whole week had passed.

We were getting ready to have a fun day at Trevor's private inlet. You heard me right. This guy bought his own inlet!

Although it wasn't surrounded by water, it was caved in by woods and out of the private eye. I was amazed at the pictures. There was a huge sandbar and then a canal of salt water perfect for swimming.

I slathered sunscreen all over my face and hurried down the stairs. "I'll be waiting in the car," Trevor announced as he walked out the front door. I followed him and carefully stepped into the backseat. Salem appeared not long after me in a new pair of swim trunks Trevor had bought him. Then we were all set.

I couldn't contain my excitement. The last time I went to a beach was with my grandma. But a private one? That sounded like luxury. My long hair whipped in the wind as Trevor rolled down his tinted windows. It was a beautiful sunny day in South Carolina, and I couldn't wait to soak up all the sun.

As soon as we arrived, I practically leapt out of the car and grabbed some beach chairs from the trunk. When I walked into the empty lot of white sand and beautiful blue water, I set down the chairs and jumped in. I could hear Salem laugh as he took his shirt off and dove in with me.

"Too cold!" I shrieked as he splashed me with water. "I can tell you kids are having fun," said Trevor as he took a sip of water. "Just don't drown on me." He winked and smiled.

The water felt amazing on a hot day like this. After some swimming, I stepped out of the water and sat down next to Trevor in a beach chair. "Nice, right?" Said Trevor. I nodded.

"It's beautiful. And private. I've never been to a private inlet before." He grinned. "We can come here anytime you want. I come here to relax when I need something to do. It's nice having some company around for once after Hudson passed away. He used to love playing in the water."

It'd been awhile since he last mentioned Hudson. I still didn't know much about him. I had so many questions, but asking a grieving father about his dead child wasn't exactly the easiest thing to do. I cleared my head and buried my feet in the sand beneath me.

Being secluded felt so good. I never wanted this to end. I couldn't ever imagine my life being like this when I was at the orphanage. It was always about sneaking out for some fresh air, or trying to finally fall asleep. The days blurred together, and things got repetitive quickly. There was no excitement. But living a life like this guaranteed something new everyday. And I loved every bit of it.

I slid on my cute pink sunglasses and watched as Salem stepped out of the water. "Dude, you bought this little beach?" Said Salem in shock.

Trevor nodded. "I'm rich. What else would I use all this money for?"

"I'm thirsty," I said as I wrapped myself in a towel. Trevor handed me a 10 dollar bill and told me to buy a drink from the vending machine a few blocks from the inlet. "Thanks," I said as I trudged through the sand and towards the parking lot. "Get me a Pepsi," Salem called after me. "Sure thing."

I grabbed a Pepsi from the vending machine and then proceeded to shove more cash through the slot. A Sprite sounded great on a hot day like this. I entered the combination and watched as the Sprite fell to the bottom with a thud.

I picked up the can and walked back to the inlet, but as I walked through the street, I couldn't help but notice the same bulletin board filled with papers and articles in front of a jewelry shop. On a Saturday, there were destined to be people everywhere.

The inlet was private, but it was located near lots of shops and restaurants typically packed with people on the weekend. I approached the bulletin board and was shocked to see a *Missing Persons* flier with my face on it. Another one? They were still searching?

At this point, I wouldn't be surprised if I was presumed dead. I tore the poster off the bulletin board and crumbled it up in my fist. Just as I was about to walk off, another newspaper caught my attention. It was plastered on the bulletin board next to my flier. *This Makes Two: Another Woman Brutally Murdered*.

I was horrified. First Felicia White, and now another woman? After skimming through the whole paper, I found some details. A forty-seven year-old woman was killed, just like Felicia had been. Her name was Deborah Stallard, and she worked at a pharmacy in Greenwood. And just like the last case, no evidence was found at the scene.

No evidence? This person knew what they were doing. I pinned the newspaper back onto the bulletin board and threw out my *Missing Persons* flier in the first trashcan I saw.

Why did they care so much about where I was? That was one less kid to worry about. Or one less teenager to be specific. No one seemed to adopt teenagers anyway. I was better off living with some rich guy I hardly knew than living in the orphanage, only to end up on the streets two years later like Salem. I took a breather and continued walking.

I reassured myself that everything was okay. That I now had a beautiful roof to live under. That Phoebe might've been adopted within these past few months. Even if she didn't, she was probably doing alright. The poster was gone. That was one less opportunity for someone to find me and turn me in.

I sighed and found my way back to the inlet, still holding the ice-cold drinks in my hand.

"There you are," said Salem as I threw him the Pepsi.

"Here's the change," I muttered. I held out the change ready to drop into Trevor's hand, but he refused. "Keep it," he muttered. "I don't need it." I thanked him and dashed back into the water with Salem after tossing the cash into my bag.

We were swimming in the water for what seemed like ages. I finally wrung out my hair and stepped out of the water for good that day.

Salem followed me onto the hot sand. We both grabbed towels and dried off. "Are you ready to go home?" I asked Trevor.

He chuckled. "You want to go home? Shouldn't we eat dinner first?" Salem and I exchanged glances with each other. "Where would we eat?"

My question got answered as soon as we pulled into the parking lot of what looked like the fanciest restaurant I had ever seen. I had since thrown clothes over my bathing suit, as did Salem and Trevor.

"This is really expensive," I gawked. Trevor winked and opened the car door for us. "It's on me, kids."

I wanted to laugh hysterically. Of course it was on him. Salem and I were practically dirt poor and would probably be living on the streets right now if it hadn't been for Trevor.

As humble of a person I was, I didn't mind stepping into such a beautifully designed restaurant like this. It wasn't everyday Salem and I got to treat ourselves after all we've been through. I was beyond grateful Trevor was helping us achieve this.

"Ah! Dr. MacQuoid. One of my favorite customers," said a gorgeous French woman wearing a black apron on top of a white polo.

"Madam Genevieve," said Trevor. "I am delighted to see you again. We would like a table for 3, please."

The woman, who was named Genevieve, instructed us to follow her to a table up a fancy spiral staircase. Chandeliers adorned the ceilings of both floors, and I was astonished by the lovely atmosphere. Diners, mostly couples of all ages, wore fancy clothes and ate 5-course meals at their tables. We finally sat in the far back of the second story.

As soon as we seated, Trevor handed us each a menu. "Order whatever you want," he said.

The food on the menu sounded delicious. I couldn't remember the last time I had a meal like anything presented on the pamphlet I was holding. It took me a few minutes to flip through it, but I finally decided.

Genevieve, the waitress, came back to our table with the drinks we had ordered and proceeded to take our food orders. "May I please have the Gnocchi Skillet with chicken, sausage, and tomatoes?" Said Trevor. "Of course," she said as she wrote down his order. "And for you, ma'am?"

I closed my menu and cleared my throat. "I'll have the Parmesan Risotto with roasted shrimp please," I said, trying my hardest to pronounce the fancy name. "And for you, young man?" She was now staring at Salem.

"I'll just have Tortellini," he mumbled. The waitress finished jotting down our orders and flashed us one more smile before disappearing into the kitchen downstairs.

"Trevor?" I asked. "Aren't our clothes a little too casual for a restaurant like this?" I bit my lip as I pointed to our cheap shirts and wrinkled bottoms.

Trevor was wearing a dressy jacket and a white polo that probably cost more than a weekly stay at our old motel.

He shook his head. "You kids look fine. Besides, it's not a crime to dress casually at a restaurant. You could say I'm pretty respected here." He smirked.

While that gave me some reassurance, I couldn't help but feel out of place. Salem and I didn't belong here. We were orphans, for Pete's sake.
My wardrobe was small, and I'm sure Salem's was, too. After all, we could only bring what fit in a backpack.

I tried not to make eye contact with any other diners for fear of judgemental looks. They were probably staring at us and whispering right now. I was startled when I heard a microphone tap, and suddenly the lights dimmed to an intimate golden color.

"What's going on?" I asked curiously. "They're getting ready to play live music," said Trevor.

A woman sashayed to the small stage in front of all the diners upstairs and was now gripping the microphone with silky gloves. Her black stilettos clacked on the sleekly stage that looked freshly

polished. She wore a beautiful red dress that matc¡
lipstick.

"Good evening everyone," she said into the microphoı
it's six o' clock, let the music begin!" There were a few ι
some of the diners and even some faint clapping. The w   .ın stood
up from her stool and as the instrumental started playing, she began
singing "We Belong Together" by Mariah Carey.

Her voice was angelic, and I would've paid just to hear her perform
alone. But I was even more excited to see our food had already
arrived at the table.

"Parmesan Risotto with roasted shrimp?" Asked Genevieve. "Right
here," I said. She set the steaming plate down in front of me and
brought out Salem and Trevor's dishes too. As soon as I took a bite,
it was easy to conclude that this was probably the best dinner I'd
ever eaten.

"How is it?" Asked Salem. "It tastes amazing," I raved. And that was
no lie. Salem began eating his Tortellini, and judging from his
shocked expression, I could tell he was amazed too.

We continued eating for another few hours. Even after finishing the
large meals, we stayed a little longer to hear the woman's
continuous live performance. After she had finally finished for the
night, we stood up from our table and left the restaurant.

"That was probably the best dinner I've had in forever", said Salem
as we got in the car. I agreed.

To be truthful, I've never had food that expensive. But that was a
comment I'd keep to myself. After all, it felt embarrassing enough
being dependent on a rich guy I'd only known for a week or so. But I
brushed it off and thanked Trevor for paying the costly bill.

on as we got home, I was ready to take a shower and crash ut. But Salem had other plans.

"It's not that late," he whined. "I want to take you somewhere." I groaned as I finished brushing my teeth. "Where?" I asked through a mouthful of toothpaste.

He grinned and twirled Trevor's car keys in his hand. "I know a place. Besides, I already told Trevor we're leaving." I rolled my eyes. "We're? I'm tired."

He sighed. "Come on, Lana. I told you to get used to this. It'll be fun, alright? Just trust me."

It was hard to say no to his pleading eyes. "Fine," I grumbled, spitting toothpaste in the sink. I grabbed my coat and untied my hair. "Surprise me."

Chapter 9:

"No," I said sternly as we pulled into the parking lot of a nightclub. "You're crazy."

He laughed. "You think I don't know that? Come on, we deserve this. So much of our lives wasted at the orphanage. Trevor's paying for everything." He flashed me a glimpse of Trevor's shiny credit card. I sighed.

As terrified as I was, Salem had a point. Didn't we deserve to have a little bit of fun every now and then? Even if we were underage. But still I sat there in the passenger seat, with my seatbelt on and a frown on my face.

As I watched Salem shut the car door and inch towards the entrance, I gave in and unbuckled my seatbelt.

A security guard was standing at the door. "Hello sir," Salem said confidently. He handed the man his ID card. "Go ahead," the man grunted. "And you, ma'am?" He was now staring at me.

"Uh . . ." I stammered, now holding up the line. "Here's her ID," said Salem. "She's with me." He nodded and let me through.

As we opened the door, I glared at him. "We're not 21. How did you get us inside?"

He pulled the two cards out of his jacket pocket and let me inspect them. "They're fake, Lana. I know a guy."

I glanced at the cards, and sure enough, they looked legit. The only difference was our names and our age, which had been changed to 21 for the sake of getting in. "How did you -" he shoved the fake IDs back into his pocket. "Let's have some fun," he whispered.

As soon as we got inside, I could practically feel other people's breaths on my back. The place was packed. Music was playing, but not the fancy, classy kind. This place reeked of alcohol.

Salem pushed his way through the crowd and I followed him like I was a child. And I was.

My heart skipped a beat as I witnessed Salem asking the bartender for a Martini.

As soon as he received his glass, he took a sip. I ran over to him, trying to avoid all the drunk people dancing around me. "Salem!" I hissed. "What are you doing?"

He took another sip from the glass and sat down at the bar. "Having a good time," he muttered. "Do you want a drink?"

I punched him in the arm. "You must be out of your mind if you think I'm going to take a sip of any cocktail. Now take me home."

He sighed. "Listen, Lana. I came here for the alcohol. Just stay by me for the rest of the night and you'll be fine. If you choose to get a drink, don't leave it unattended. Ever. You hear me?"

My mouth dropped. "I don't have to hear you because I'm not touching a drink, Salem. You have to take me home at some point, so don't you dare drink more than a glass." I was beyond overwhelmed. But I deserved to have a good time, too. Despite hearing Salem call after me as I wandered away from him, I continued walking until I found a more quiet place to sit, farther away from the crowd. Deep breaths, I told myself. *Deep breaths.*

I looked around, as if hoping to recognize someone. Who was I kidding? I was a runaway orphan from the next city over. Of course I didn't know anyone but Salem.

Then my attention drove from the random people in the crowd to someone in particular. I recognized a face. The blonde hair. The fair skin. It was the same guy I somehow kept running into. What was he doing here? And what were the chances I'd see him *again*?

Naturally, I tried my best to avoid him because of my paranoid state. But the more I saw him appear throughout the night, the closer I studied him. Something I hadn't noticed before was the small tattoo he had on his neck, exposed by the bright beams of light that changed colors. I tried to make out what the tattoo was, but it was hard to tell as he swayed to the beat of the music amongst the wild crowd. A bird? I squinted. A yellow bird? It was a canary. But why did he tattoo a canary on his neck?

I brushed off the encounter and tried to ignore the guy with the canary tattoo. I wasn't gonna lie, having a shot or two sounded fun in the moment. But I knew one of us had to stay sober, and clearly it wasn't going to be Salem.

"Excuse me, ma'am. What time is it?" I now found myself asking a drunk woman. She looked at me and laughed in a drunken state. I rolled my eyes and pushed past her.

"Sir? What time is it?" I asked another man. He glanced at his watch. "10:29 P.M.," he said. I was starting to get worried.

I felt humiliated walking around a nightclub without holding a drink in my hand. Almost everyone I had seen was drinking some form of alcohol, whether it be from a plastic red cup or a shot glass. The music grew louder as more people began to pour inside. It felt like my walls were caving in.

Eventually, I reached the dance floor and decided to loosen up a little; only without alcohol. I swayed my hips a little and pretended like I knew the song the DJ was playing. I surely looked out of place, and even though my heart was thumping rapidly, I tried to use my adrenaline to power me through.

I threw my arms up like everyone else, but most of them were a lot older and tipsy. They looked like they were having a lot more fun than I was.

After realizing I wasn't going to have that same giddy feeling, I felt a little discouraged and dropped my arms. And when I felt a hand graze my hips, I left the dance floor for good.

I was starting to get tired. "Lonely No More" By Rob Thomas was now playing on the loudspeakers. I decided to go look for Salem after starting to hear all the soppy music, so I headed over to the barstool I last saw him at. He wasn't there.

"Salem?" I asked, barely able to even hear myself. I groaned. Where was he?

"Salem?" I called out again, now shoving past people with hostility. "Hello?"

"Excuse me sir. Have you seen a tall, lean guy with dark hair and a deep voice?" I frantically asked someone. He shook his head, understandably. My description of him probably fit any other eighteen year old man taking shots in this place.

"Salem!" I was panicking. I was now receiving one dirty look after another as I pushed past people. My heart relaxed a little as I finally spotted him.

"Salem Coleman! How much did you have to drink?" I yelled as I stormed over to him. He was standing shirtless, and appeared to be flirting with some old woman. Seriously, she looked to be in her late fifties.

"You're taking me back to Trevor's and we're leaving." The woman scrunched her nose as she saw me. I pulled Salem away from her and practically dragged him by the ear out to the car. "Hey, what are we -"

I finally let go of him now that we were standing in the parking lot. "Look at you! Where is your shirt?" I asked him. "Why did you take it off in the first place?"

He was still unfazed with all the shots he had downed. "It was hot in there." I rolled my eyes.

His dark hair was ruffled and his eyes were bloodshot. He looked at me and offered me a smile, but it wasn't the smile I was used to.

"Are you fit to drive?" I asked hesitantly. "Yeah, just . . . get in the car," he slurred. He stumbled forward as he took another step; beer splashing out of the cup he was still grasping. "Salem! We're finding a Taxi."

He shook his head. "I just tripped. I'm perfectly fit to drive." He was slurring his words badly now.

"You're not fit to drive. I can't believe you let this happen," I grumbled. He looked at me with confusion. "Let what happen?"

I looked at him in disbelief. "This!" I yelled. "I mean, look at you. You were flirting with some lady who's old enough to be your mom and you somehow managed to lose your shirt while you were at it."

He laughed. "Where's my cigarettes? I just want one before we leave," he said, now pulling a lighter out of his pocket.

"We're leaving now, and you're not touching another cigarette until you're sober." I felt like I was talking to a child. I was practically embarrassed for him as a couple other people stood in the parking lot, watching him laugh and stumble.

I finally managed to get Salem in the car. As he slid his red cup in the cup holder of Trevor's car, I grabbed it and furiously tossed the cup into the parking lot, beer now spilling out on the street.

"Hey, I was drinking that." I wanted to burst out laughing. "It's bad enough that you're driving drunk. There's no way in hell I'd let you take another sip of that." I glanced over at the beer cup I had thrown.

Although he certainly wasn't fit to drive, we had no cash for a Taxi and I wouldn't dare touch the steering wheel myself.

"Dude. You're driving one of Trevor's luxury cars," I exclaimed. "If you wreck it, he'd probably kill us both."

Saying I was petrified was an understatement. I took a deep breath for what seemed like the tenth time that night and strapped my seatbelt on with shaky hands. Still disoriented, he turned the keys in the ignition and the car engine roared. "Drive," I breathed.

Chapter 10:

We were now pulling out of the parking lot. The small clock on the dashboard read 12:09 A.M. With trembling hands, Salem turned the steering wheel and we jerked out of the parking spot.

The whole drive was nauseating. Salem hadn't even remembered what Trevor's address was. The tension was filled everytime I yelled, "Stop!" or, "Slow down!" when he went too fast.

My main concern was Trevor. I wanted to call him, and explain the situation. That Salem was drunk out of his wits. That he was now speeding down the street in a car that costs more than any of my old foster homes combined. That he needed to pick us up if I wanted to feel safe.

But if I did this, what if Trevor kicked us out? What if he deemed us as "too irresponsible" to drive his car anywhere? Or worse, what if we got into legal trouble because we were underage? I didn't want to risk it. "Keep driving," I said as calmly as I could. "You're doing alright."

"Dude!" I cried as we swerved right. "We almost crashed into a tree!"

He slowed the car down and sighed. "I'm sorry. I'm just, a little, uh . . . tipsy," he said through breaths.

"It's okay, Salem." I gently patted him on the shoulder. I could tell even through his drunk voice that he felt bad he had put me in this situation. But I understood. He made a mistake and drank too much, but that was just his way of expressing his freedom. That's all he ever wanted at the orphanage, and I knew giving him a hard time in the car right now was not going to get us home any safer. "You're doing alright," I repeated. "Keep driving, we're almost to Trevor's."

We were getting close to Trevor's neighborhood when the car swerved left. Thank god the road was deserted at this time, because this could've easily caused an accident.

"What are you doing?" I panicked. He pulled the car over to the side of the road and unbuckled his seatbelt. "Salem?"

He didn't answer. Instead, he hopped out of the car and stumbled to the woods. I rolled down the driver's window to see what he was doing, but as I saw him hunched over, I knew. He was throwing up.

I rolled up the window and tried not to look too disgusted because I knew he drank too much and couldn't help it. As soon as he got back in the car, he acted as if nothing happened. "Are you okay?" I asked with unease.

"Perfectly fine," he assured me. But I could tell he still felt sick. He started up the car and drove off; a little too fast to be safe.

Relief washed over me as we finally pulled into Trevor's driveway. Lucky for us, Trevor's huge mansion was easy to spot considering how big it was.

Salem slowed the car down and put it in park. He opened the door and was about to step out when he lurched forward. I hurried over to his side and helped steady him. "Let me help you," I said. "But when we walk inside, you have to act as sober as possible in front of Trevor." The last thing I needed was for Trevor to realize we were at a nightclub underage while Salem almost crashed his Porsche.

I rang the doorbell, still helping Salem to the door. It was dead of night and Salem was practically swaying. "Hang in there," I muttered under my breath.

It took a minute, but Trevor opened the door. "Hi Trevor," I said, trying to hide my exhaustion and frustration from tonight. He grinned and let us inside.

"Whatever you kids were up to, did you have fun?" He asked, now sitting in the kitchen.

"Yeah," I said. "Lots of fun." I nervously smiled and walked Salem upstairs so he could go to bed. As soon as Trevor was out of sight, I snapped my fingers.

"Salem, I know you're tired. But we're almost to the bed. Keep walking." He opened his eyes wider and carefully stepped over each of the glossy stairs.

When we made it to Hudson's empty room, Salem traipsed over to the bed and collapsed as soon as he pulled back the covers. "Goodnight," I laughed, now letting it sink in that the two of us had made it home safe after such a night. He had already passed out.

I walked back downstairs where Trevor was because, surprisingly, I was wide awake. "Is Salem already asleep?" He asked. I nodded. "He was pretty tired." And drunk.

"So anyways, what did you guys do tonight?" Trevor asked while pouring coffee into a glass mug. Oh god. I tried to think of the best excuse I could. "We went for a walk on the beach," I asserted. He furrowed his brow. "Which beach?"

Great. Was that the best lie I could come up with? "Some beach nearby; I'm not sure what it was called. Anyways, I should probably get ready for bed too. Thanks for letting us borrow your car." Even though we almost crashed it.

He took another sip of his coffee. "Anytime, Lana. Goodnight." I hurried up the stairs before he could interrogate me. But I guess I wasn't fast enough, because I heard his voice again.

"Did Salem enjoy all those shots?"

I froze. "What?"

"The nightclub. How was it?"

I cautiously walked back down the stairs. "How - how did you know?"

"Ah, kid. You think I wasn't a teenager once? I know all the mannerisms. I'm a psychiatrist," he laughed.

Right. "I hope you're not mad -"

He shook his head. "Of course not. I'm glad you guys had fun. Just be careful, okay? Boy, he's gonna wake up with a nasty hangover tomorrow."

"Yeah. Well, thanks Trevor. Goodnight," I said, feeling both confused and relieved. With how many shots Salem had, I forgot how obvious it looked.

When I stepped inside Hudson's bedroom, the first thing I noticed was the fake IDs we had used that night sitting on the floor. They must've fallen out of Salem's pocket as he crawled into bed.

I picked them up and stared at my fake ID card. It was funny seeing such a realistic looking ID that was one hundred percent fake.

Seeming as I wasn't ready for bed just yet, I went over to my bag sitting on the floor and dug through it so I could find my real ID card.

I wanted to compare the fake one to the real one to see how similar they were. But when I pulled out my wallet, it wasn't there. Strange. I checked all the pockets in the purple wallet, but it was nowhere to be seen.

I always kept it in here just in case I needed it. So why was it missing?

I continued searching through all my stuff; even Salem's because I was desperate. I hadn't used my real ID card anywhere for weeks. It couldn't have just vanished.

After several minutes of searching, I decided it wasn't the end of the world. Sure, someone could've found it and possibly even turned it into the police if they knew who I was. But the chances of that happening were very slim.

It's not like I'd need it anywhere anytime soon. Besides, I didn't want to wake Salem. Not that he would wake up, because he was passed out. I yawned and put myself at ease over my missing ID. I'm sure it'll appear at some point tomorrow, and it'd be easier to find when it was bright outside.

My day today was exhausting, but at least I wasn't the one who would wake up with a hangover tomorrow. I glanced at Salem. He was definitely going to regret drinking that much when the sun rose. I just hoped it wouldn't be too rough on him.

Chapter 11:

It was already noon. I woke up early because I had trouble sleeping from the previous night. Salem however, was still asleep.

I checked on him every once in a while to make sure he was okay, as this was abnormally long for someone like him to sleep for. But I just blamed it on the alcohol.

"Wanna go anywhere today?" Asked Trevor. I shrugged. If I was being honest, I was still drained from last night. Staying in Trevor's mansion and relaxing sounded like a great way to spend my Sunday.

"Actually, I think it's better if we just stayed home today. Unless you want to go somewhere specific." He looked nervous. On edge. I had no idea why, but that was none of my business. I went back upstairs to check on Salem again. He was still out cold.

As soon as I walked into the kitchen, I noticed a newspaper sitting on the counter by the sink. *Body Discovered In Greenwood; Killer Remains Unfound* was what the title read. Another murder? In the same city? This would make three. And they were all young women.

I continued reading the newspaper. According to the article, a young woman named Serenity Hall had been missing for months. Her husband, Jack Hall, was the prime suspect up until a few weeks ago.

Her body was discovered in an alleyway not far from home in Greenwood. She had a son named Kyle, and my heart ached for him. Whoever had committed the despicable crime was still not clear.

I put the paper down where I had found it before Trevor got back to the kitchen. I just hoped they would find the killer soon and put them behind bars so Serenity, Felicia, and Debbie would all get justice. That was, if they had all been murdered by the same person.

Still beat, I decided to make some coffee. I wasn't the usual coffee-type of person, but then again, I was so used to the watered down coffee we occasionally received at the orphanage. I'd rather drink tap water than touch that coffee.

"Trevor, could I make a cup of coffee?" I asked him. After all, it was his kitchen. "Allow me to make it for you," he said with a smile. He walked into the kitchen and grabbed a mug.

"You sure?" I asked while drinking a glass of water. "Of course."

When he handed me the coffee, I took a sip. It instantly took me back to when I was little, and I tried coffee for the first time. My grandma had made coffee like this all the time, and it was my favorite. There was no doubt this coffee tasted amazing.

"My head is pounding." I turned around to see Salem, who was now standing behind me. "Salem!" I said, jumping out of my chair. I went to give him a hug. "Woah," he said, almost toppling backwards as I tackled him.

He hugged me back, but stopped and rubbed his temples. "Are you okay?" I asked, concerned.

"I'm fine. Just a little exhausted." Trevor walked over to him. "What happened?"

I couldn't tell if Salem was covering up his party animal habits from last night on purpose or if he genuinely couldn't remember a thing, because he answered, "I'm not sure. I'm a little dizzy."

I pretended to not have a clue as to why he was in this state, but he was most definitely hung over, and maybe even a little buzzed. "Sit down," I said. But instead, he grabbed a bottle of water and headed towards the door.

"Where are you going?" I asked as he slipped on his sneakers. "Gas station," he murmured.

"Why?" He opened the front door. "I'm gonna need a lot of cigarettes to kill this headache."

I couldn't believe him. "There's Aspirin for that. Or Ibuprofen." I hurriedly headed over to the kitchen and opened all the cabinets until I found the right bottles. "Here," I said as I poured the whole bottle of Aspirin into my hand. "Take these."

Salem frowned. "Put those back. I don't need painkillers. I'll be back in a few." Just great. This wasn't good for him at all. I couldn't let this become a habit.

"Stop!" I yelled as I stepped outside. "Salem, seriously. You don't need cigarettes. They're horrible for you."

As I went to rush after him, Trevor grabbed my arm. "Lana, let the boy get his cigarettes. You only live once, you know."

I grimaced. "But he's underage anyway. Aren't you well respected in this city? Surely *you* of all people would enforce the law."

He laughed. "He's still a legal adult. You're still young."

I shook my head. "I'm sixteen. We're only two years apart. I'm just looking out for my friend, okay? He's practically all I have." Trevor grimaced after my statement.

Although I didn't want Salem to touch the cigarettes, I knew I couldn't prevent him from doing anything. Trevor was right when he said Salem was an adult, and could make his own decisions. But he was wrong about me being young. I was mature for my age. I was almost an adult, and I had certainly been through enough to say I had some sort of background.

I headed for the stairs. I needed time to cool off. I didn't want my best friend to end up on one of those smoking prevention commercials in a few years. I could just imagine him with gray hairs and that raspy, hoarse voice at age thirty. The thought sent a shiver down my spine.

It had been several minutes, and Salem still wasn't back. I didn't feel the need to worry, because, well - it was Salem. I knew he'd be fine no matter the circumstances. Maybe he was just taking his time. It was one o' clock.

More time had passed, and he still wasn't back. "Wanna watch a movie?" Trevor asked as I sat on the couch in the living room. "Sure, why not?" I said sharply, still a little annoyed at his comment.

I figured there was nothing better to do than to sit down and watch a movie. Movies are relaxing, right? That's exactly what I needed.

"What do you wanna watch?" Asked Trevor as he grabbed the remote off his fancy coffee table. I had no idea. It'd been a long time since I had last watched a movie. Usually we watched them at the orphanage on a single TV that we all had to crowd around, so movie experiences weren't all that. But Trevor's nice TV would be much different. Just like the coffee.

"You can pick a movie," I said. He settled on a random action movie I had never seen before, but I was more into comedies. He pressed play and we began watching.

I pretended to be intrigued throughout the first few scenes, but as the movie progressed, I found myself losing interest. My mind was dead set on Salem and why he was taking so long to buy a pack of cigarettes.

"I don't feel good," I lied to get out of the movie. I stood up and brushed myself off. "I think I'll head upstairs."

Trevor continued watching the movie, and I kept my word. Even though it'd been weeks now, it was still awkward when it was just Trevor and me.

I didn't want to go back downstairs until Salem was home. But part of me was still worried about him. He did have a killer headache, after all.

I assumed he was fine. I worried way too much. Without a second thought, I eventually fell asleep in bed, despite it being the middle of a sunny day. It felt nice getting some peaceful sleep after so much tossing and turning from the night before. I couldn't really remember much after that.

I was basically drowning in my thoughts as I dreamt of wild dreams throughout my sleep. I was in the middle of being chased by cops after robbing a gas station in this one. There were the sirens, blaring as I made my way through the rest of an unfamiliar town. That was, until I woke up in a cold sweat.

Something wasn't right here. *The sirens*. If I was awake, why were the sirens still playing in my head? Only, they weren't all in my head. I realized this after I heard Trevor storm to the front door as red and blue lights were flashing through the window of the bedroom I was in.

What was going on? Panicked, I hurried downstairs despite having just woken up and followed Trevor to the front door. A tall officer dashed to the porch. "Police!" He yelled.

Startled, I froze. The officer's face lit up as soon as he saw me. "Lana Garcia! You're alive. We were just about to close this case until we received an anonymous tip. She's here!" He yelled to another officer, now standing on the patio of Trevor's mansion.

I was at a loss for words. I couldn't process this. "What are you talking about?" I asked.

"We've received new information regarding your kidnapping case. A tall, lanky man with brown hair was caught on surveillance footage escorting you out of an orphanage on that very morning you disappeared. We received some tips on this case by an anonymous caller who directed us to this address."

I coughed. Salem? The *kidnapper*?

Salem was not a kidnapper. It was bad enough I was caught despite having a low profile. It was even worse that my best friend who pulled me out of my miserable life at the orphanage was being called my kidnapper.

The officer, who introduced himself as Deputy Miller, continued. "After investigating the orphanage, they were able to pull up all the information we needed to identify your captor. His name is Salem Coleman, he is eighteen years old, and he was aged out of the orphanage the day of your disappearance. Police are out searching for him now. In the meantime, we're going to take you to the station for proper questioning."

I didn't want to go. Anything to do with the police sent the alarms in my head sounding. But I couldn't refuse.

"And as for you, Dr. MacQuoid. It is a pleasure seeing you again. Do you have any insight on this case? What is your relation to Lana Garcia?"

Trevor was dumbfounded, yet stayed professional. "Hello, Deputy Miller. I am not related to Lana Garcia or Salem Coleman in any way. I picked the two of them up in my car after they needed a ride. After hearing they needed a place to stay, I was more than happy to let them stay with me. I have dealt with many patients in the past suffering from mental illnesses due to being in foster care. I had no idea Mister Coleman had kidnapped Lana. If I had known this sooner, I would've come forward with this sensitive information."

I tried my best to contain myself. "Salem didn't kidnap me. He was an orphan too. I chose to run away with him. Please, don't get him in trouble. He's innocent." I was pleading.

Thank god Salem hadn't come back yet, or else he would've been detained already. "Whatever you do Salem, do not come back here until the police are out of this mess," I cursed under my breath.

"This case is more complex than we thought. Miss Garcia, please follow me for questioning. We will keep Dr. MacQuoid updated. Remember, you are safe with us."

Was that Trevor's last name? It was the first time I had heard of it.

"Where are we going?" I asked as I was ushered into the back of a police car. Deputy Miller shut the door as I put my seatbelt on. "To the police station."

Chapter 12:

The whole trip with the two officers in the front seat was dead silent, but I didn't mind this. It's not like I wanted to be brought to the police station so I could be questioned about the "kidnapping case" that didn't actually exist.

As soon as we pulled into the station, I got out of the car as Deputy Miller opened the door. With my heart beating rapidly, I trembled to the entrance.

"Am I in trouble?" I asked.

Deputy Miller laughed. "You're not in trouble. You are the victim. We are going to ask you different questions so we can hear your side of the story. Now please step inside the lobby and wait for assistance. We will have a detective speak with you to receive a better understanding of what action will be taken." I nodded hesitantly.

A few minutes had passed, and I found myself scared out of my wits. I was on my own in a police station.

I didn't belong here. Salem didn't belong here. Where was he, anyway? Usually I'd be worried for him, but this time I was glad he was out of sight. Getting caught by the police would make this situation so much worse than it already was.

He had most likely seen the police at Trevor's and took off. He was a smart guy. Despite not having the best education, he wasn't stupid. I was sure he'd dealt with police before, as he didn't have the best reputation. And buying cigarettes and alcohol with a fake ID didn't help his case either.

I prayed he was okay. I felt so vulnerable when he was away. But why did I feel like this? I shouldn't be depending on someone else, but I couldn't help it. Was I going *crazy*?

"Lana Garcia," I heard a voice call from the hallway. "Please follow me to the interrogation room."

I did as I was told and followed the man inside a small, plain room with a round wooden table in the middle. The man took a seat.

"Allow me to introduce myself," he stated. "I am a former detective in this county. One of my many jobs here is to interview suspects when crime cases are brought to light. You, of course, are not a suspect. Let me make that very clear. I know you're young, and you're probably scared. But don't worry. I am only here to ask you simple questions about what happened during your disappearance, and what you know about your captor. My name is Lars Lablanc, but you can call me Detective Lars."

I couldn't stand when he called my best friend my captor. But I had to keep my comments to myself. I would speak my side when asked to. In this case, I had a lot to say if I wanted to clear Salem's name.

"Okay, Lana. Before you speak, I am required to let you know that you are being recorded on a surveillance camera. There is also a voice audio microphone right in the middle of this table." He was now pointing to a small device planted in between us as we sat across from each other.

"Whatever you say will be recorded. You do have the right to stay silent if you do not feel comfortable answering the questions I ask. Remember, do not lie. Do not sugarcoat anything. We are here to help you. With that being said, let me ask you the first question. What is your full name?"

I couldn't make eye contact. "Lana Cecilia Garcia."

Lars nodded, and jotted my name down on a notepad. "Great job Lana. Now for the next question. What do you recall happened when you and Salem Coleman exited the orphanage a few months ago?" I could already tell this was going to take awhile.

"Well," I began. "Salem was my best friend at the orphanage. We did everything together. So when I realized he was being aged out now that he was an adult, I was devastated.

I didn't want to be alone anymore, and at this point, I accepted the fact that I was most likely never going to find my forever family. As soon as he hurried out the front door, I followed him without thinking until he finally agreed to let me stay with him. And that's why we were rushing out the door on the day I went missing. I was chasing him." I swallowed and caught my breath.

He briefly summarized everything I had just said on paper. "And you're positive he did not force you or persuade you to run away with him?"

I nodded. "Positive."

He grunted. "And Salem Coleman - he did not threaten you in any way that he would harm you or someone you loved if you didn't run away with him?"

"No. Of course not."

"Okay, Lana. Remember, you do not have to cover for him. Do not lie about any of this. You're speaking the truth?"

"Yes sir."

"Moving on. Did you and Salem have a romantic, intimate relationship with each other?"

"Oh, god no. We're best friends. I love him, but not like that. He's like - a big brother to me."

"Has he ever physically or mentally abused you, Lana?"

"No. He would never. Never has, never will. You've got to believe me," I pleaded.

"Relax. Everything you say will be used as evidence. I am not accusing you of lying. I have to ask you these questions regardless of how crazy they sound in order to dive deeper into this case."

I took a deep breath. "Next question please."

I had a long, detailed conversation with Detective Lars after that. As uncomfortable as I was, I kept my composure and reminded myself of my morals. I answered every question truthfully and tensely watched him take notes.

"Alright, Lana. We are going to end this interview with one final question. How would you feel if Salem Coleman was sent to federal prison if found guilty for holding you captive? And why?"

I shook my head. "You don't understand. Salem is innocent. I'd be devastated if he served any jail time for committing something he didn't do.

I'm not a victim. I'm a stupid teenager who selfishly ran away with him even after knowing he could potentially get in trouble for it. I take accountability for that. But please, this isn't Salem's fault. He was trying to help me."

Lars sighed. "There's clearly two very different sides to the story here. We will be analyzing all of the evidence we have on this case and more.

Now, I know I said after that last question that this interview would be ended. But I must ask you this - do you or do you not know where Salem Coleman is right now?"

I rubbed my temples vigorously. This was all just so hard to process. How was I supposed to answer this question? Should I lie and simply tell Lars I had no idea? To be fair, this was partially true. The last time I had heard from him was this morning when he announced he was going to the gas station for cigarettes. Now that the police were searching for him, he could be anywhere.

Or I could be honest and tell him exactly what I knew. Instead of going for either of these choices, I blurted, "I don't want to answer this question."

Lars paused for a moment before furrowing his brow. "May I ask if there's any reason that you do not want to answer this question?" He queried.

I shrugged. "I don't feel comfortable answering this question, sir. I would rather stay silent." I could tell he was not amused of my answer. But technically, I wasn't doing anything wrong by not answering a question.

"Thank you for your time with me today, Lana," said Lars. "I am going to ask you to wait in the lobby until we make some phone calls to arrange your temporary placement." I followed him out to the lobby and took a seat.

I was already exhausted, and the sun hadn't even set yet. But now, I had another problem on my hands. Who was I going to stay with?

Anywhere but the orphanage. There was no going back there.

Almost an hour had passed, and a sheriff stepped into the lobby. "Lana," he said. "We have decided it is best if you stayed with Dr. MacQuoid, as he is a psychiatrist. He has gladly offered to take you in and even help you fix your mental state. If you know what I mean." He smiled nervously.

"Actually, I don't know what you mean." I glared at him, confused. "What is that supposed to mean?"

He cleared his throat. "Just get in the police car so I can drive you home before it gets dark. I can explain more on the way."

I was now sitting in the back of a police car for the second time that day.

"So," I exclaimed. "Are you going to evaluate a little on my *mental state*?"

The officer, who still didn't give me a name, coughed. "Well, Lana. Judging from your interview, we feel it is best to send you to someone far more experienced to make sure you're not mentally damaged or scarred. We don't want to evaluate this evidence until we're sure it's coming directly from your brain, and not something else."

I was stunned. "So, you're basically saying I'm crazy?" I laughed to shield my anger and disbelief.

"No, Lana. It's not like that. It's just -" I stopped him. "You told me that the information I gave you regarding my own story wasn't coming from the brain? That's correct?"

The officer pulled into Trevor's driveway. "You're getting defensive. Dr. MacQuoid is a trusted man in our county, and we hold him to very high standards. If anyone is able to give us a direct answer as to what we should look out for, it's him. Besides, you were staying with him before this. You'll be fine." Was he being serious?

Trevor wasn't my issue here. I was insulted and appalled that the police officers I looked to for guidance were convinced I was insane. They asked for the truth, and I gave it to them raw. I knew myself better than anyone else, and I was confident I didn't need any sort of confirmation, even if this confirmation was coming from someone with a fancy title. The officer opened the door and helped me out of the car.

"Dr. MacQuoid has promised to keep us updated on how you're doing. In the meantime, don't stress yourself out. You're a smart girl." The officer grinned.

"And remember, don't disclose any legal information to anyone but Dr. MacQuoid. Don't trust anybody else, and make sure to come to the station or phone us right away if you have any new information. Have a good night, kiddo." I closed the door and walked up to Trevor's porch.

As soon as he let me inside, I felt relieved. We weren't incredibly close, but I guess we had to bond somehow while Salem was still missing in action. This was going to be a challenge considering he was now juggling the role of being my psychiatrist and my legal guardian. I just hoped things would work out in the end. And most importantly, fingers crossed that Salem was safe, and not partying somewhere downing one shot after another.

I sighed heavily. Having a wild imagination was fun and all, but not when you were stuck in a midlife crisis; and missing your best friend who could possibly end up going to jail because of you.

Chapter 13:

"Hello, Lana." Said Trevor, now sitting next to me on the sofa. "I have no patients to see this week. I have reserved this whole week so we could have a chat. I know this is a lot to grasp, but I promise you, I will work with you and help you to my best ability." He grunted. "Just remember, you have to be honest and truthful with me. Our first session officially starts tomorrow morning. In the meantime, I want you to process everything that's happened today so you don't get overwhelmed. I don't care what you do. Let me know if there's anything I can do to make you feel more comfortable."

He stood up and headed to the kitchen. "Do you want anything to eat?" He asked. I appreciated his kindness, but I had completely lost my appetite because of the fear I was feeling. "No thanks," I sighed.

A few hours had passed, and I found myself watching a random movie on Trevor's TV. I was trying to pay attention, but all my mind wanted to know was where the hell Salem was.

Was he at a bar? He didn't have much stuff with him, I assumed, because all of his belongings aside from his wallet were still in our room. He was on the run from police. But how much more running could he do?

Probably a lot. I was sure he'd been on the run from cops before. He had experience. But being on the run for serious allegations like kidnapping was much different from the usual shoplifting or drinking underage. Did he even know what he was on the run for?

Clearly he was innocent, and it was obvious he didn't kidnap or abuse me. If only he knew why the police were after him. Would he be mad at *me*?

Anyone would be shocked if they were falsely accused of kidnapping someone, or worse. My heart ached for him. I vowed to do whatever I possibly could to keep him out of trouble. After all, he didn't deserve any of this. Neither of us did.

I paused the TV and approached the front door. "Where are you going?" Asked Trevor as I slipped on my shoes. "Just for a walk around the city," I said. I just wanted some fresh air so I could clear my mind.

"I'm sorry, Lana. But the authorities have asked me to keep you here while they're searching for Salem, and investigating. In the meantime, they have instructed you to stay inside."

I rolled my eyes. "Why? He's not a threat. He's not my kidnapper. I was never held captive. Besides, I wouldn't go far."

"Not my rules. If you're looking for something to do, go look around and see what you can find. I have everything you could possibly need here. There's some offices, a gym, and tons of other cool rooms upstairs. If you're hungry, find something to eat. Just make yourself at home, okay?" He reassured me. "Tomorrow morning we'll start your therapy."

What Trevor didn't know was that he was wasting his time trying to *help* me. I didn't need therapy. I didn't need to talk to someone about my "mental state". What I really needed was an actual family. Somewhere I could call my home, and it surely wasn't the orphanage. I didn't want foster parents who just wanted money from the government. Was that so much to ask for?

Frustrated, I went upstairs and spent the rest of my time doing random things with whatever I could find in Trevor's mansion.

"Lana, wake up." I rubbed my eyes and got up from the sofa I had managed to somehow fall asleep in.

"Morning? Already?" I said, flustered. "What room is this?" I looked around to see bookcases, a desk, a TV, and collectibles hanging on the walls.

"This is my office," said Trevor. "I guess you fell asleep here." How embarrassing. "Sorry."

He chuckled. "Nothing to be sorry about. I'm glad you're already feeling more at home." I wanted to blurt, "I don't have a home." But then again, this mansion was kind of like my home until things got sorted.

"Anyways, it's about time we have a little chat." I glared at him, unamused. "My therapy session so you can make sure I'm not insane. You could've just put it that way." He tried to keep the smile he had on his face upright. "Follow me into a private office," he advised. How many offices did he need?

We stepped into an office that was in the far back of the second story. It was plain, but decorated with little messages and bright colors that supposedly were there to uplift people. Clearly it didn't work on me, because my glum and moody expression was still easy to read.

"Have a seat," said Trevor. I sat down on the comfy leather chair across from him.

"So, what exactly are we going to do?" I asked. He grabbed out a notepad, just like Detective Lars had when he prepared for my interview. "Not another interview," I pleaded. He gave a breathy laugh.

"Lana, relax. I'm not going to be interviewing you. It's my job as a psychiatrist to recognize and identify your problems. It has been made clear that you are facing a dilemma that must be addressed by someone like me.

Everything you tell me will be staying between us for the sake of your privacy, so that shouldn't be a concern. Let me know if there's anything I can do to make you feel situated."

He took his seat and typed something on the large desktop in front of him. With his pen in hand, he cleared his throat. "First of all, I just want to let you know that this office is where we will be meeting for the next few days. I usually see my patients at an actual office, but given the circumstances here, it would make more sense to do this in the comfort of our home." I noted that he said *our* home instead of his. What was that supposed to mean? It's not like I paid rent here.

"Okay, Lana. So tell me how you and Salem met each other."

I thought for a moment. "Salem was admitted into the orphanage at a young age. When I was tossed into the orphanage, the two of us met on the very first day I had arrived. We hit it off and instantly clicked.

From that day on, we did almost everything together, and when he was finally aged out of the system, I convinced him to let me run away with him. I couldn't bear the thought of being without him. He was the best thing that could've happened to me."

I smiled just thinking about the two of us and the adventures we had been on throughout all these rough months.

Trevor wrote everything I had said in the notepad. "Perfect. And are you sure that he did not force you to do anything you didn't want to do throughout this so-called friendship?"

Alarmed, I stayed silent for a moment before coming to his defense. "What do you mean so-called? We were best friends. It's not like he just scooped me up from the orphanage and took off." He nodded.

"So you, Lana, are claiming that Salem Coleman did not kidnap you?" He asked.

"That's exactly right."

Trevor continued. "Have you ever been put in a situation that has left you traumatized or scarred as of recently?"

I took a deep breath. "The last time I was mentally scarred was when I was put up for adoption. I didn't want my environment to change, and I didn't want to leave what little family I had left.

Salem had shown the kindness I needed to be in the right mindset. He helped me get through this transition. The two of us could relate to each other because he had been put in the same situation. That's why we have such a strong bond."

Trevor looked at me suspiciously. "So, you feel you can relate to him because he assured you he was in the same boat?" He pressed.

"Basically."

"If Salem was taken away from you, and you never saw him again, how would you recover from that?"

"I wouldn't," I shrugged.

"And how do you feel about the police trying to put him in prison?"

I shuddered. "I would do everything in my power to avoid that."

"Now, Lana. I'm not saying there will be a court case regarding this, but if there was to be, would you or would you not testify against Salem?"

"I would never testify against him," I stated as clearly as I could. "He isn't a criminal."

"Now, if I told you the police were helping you by imprisoning Salem Coleman, would you or would you not believe me?"

"I wouldn't believe you."

Trevor took a few minutes to continue writing down our conversation. "You're doing good, Lana. I have your personal record and police notes pulled up on my computer. It states that you and

Salem were originally from North Augusta. Why did you two leave North Augusta, and whose decision was it?"

"It was my decision. I had no interest going back to the orphanage, so moving to an entirely different city to avoid being seen was the best option for us. Salem simply agreed and we moved the next day, but he didn't force me or pressure me to move here. If anything, it was the other way around." I swallowed and prayed what I was saying didn't sound too out of order, even though it was true.

"I've gotten a lengthy amount of notes so far. I'd say I have everything I need on this notepad to move on to the next step of your therapy, which is when I go over symptoms of potential mental illnesses. Don't get scared. Remember, I am here to help you. We all are." And with that, he put the pen and notepad in a secure drawer and stood.

"I don't want to rush this process, so I think that just about sums it up for today. If you want more coffee, I can brew some." He walked out the door and I did the same.

I made my way to the kitchen. I was starving, and I wasn't eating all that much lately. I went over to the pantry to find something to eat when I stumbled across a full bottle of champagne.

The bottle had to have cost a fortune. It was a beautifully crafted glass bottle, decorated with hearts and ribbons. The actual champagne was still inside, and the bottle looked untouched. Upon closer inspection, there was a little card attached. I squinted to read what it said.

To my beloved husband. I hope you have a great Valentine's Day. I love you.

This had to be an old bottle. Whoever this was from clearly wasn't around anymore. I disregarded the tag and, feeling daring, popped open the bottle.

I'd never tried alcohol before, and maybe it wasn't my place to open such a bottle, but Salem had been drinking it for years. Couldn't *I* have a little fun?

Even though the bottle was Trevor's, I grabbed a glass from the cupboard and poured some champagne. Within the first sip, I gagged. It was too sour for my taste buds.

I spit it out in the sink and dumped the rest of the glass down the drain.

"Lana, what are you doing?" It was Trevor.

I turned around, glass still in my hand, and tried not to look as freaked out as I was. He spotted the now open bottle on the counter next to me and frowned. "Is that champagne? You drink this stuff?" He was now glaring at me.

"No! I was just curious. Actually, this is my first time trying alcohol, and it'll probably be my last. It tasted awful to me. I should probably stop talking now. Listen Trevor, I'm sorry -" he stopped me. "I'm not mad."

I paused. "You're not?"

He sighed. "I know you're sixteen, and most kids your age like to experiment with all sorts of things. But I don't want to see you go down that path. Let's put this away." He went to grab the bottle, but stopped abruptly. "Is that -" he looked closer. "Where did you find this?"

I pointed to the pantry. "It was hidden." His expression changed immediately and, almost like instinct, he tossed the whole bottle into the garbage.

"Why did you just toss expensive champagne?" I asked.

"I thought I got rid of that ages ago. Find something to eat and don't touch any alcohol. Better yet, stop experimenting with things that aren't yours." He stormed out of the kitchen with clenched fists. Why did he get so angry after seeing that bottle?

"Noted."

Chapter 14:

I was left alone in the living room watching another movie. Now that I was stuck in the house because I was supposedly "kidnapped", the options on how to kill time were limited. I just hoped this would all subside.

Ever since Trevor caught me with the champagne, I was left feeling worse than ever.

It was a dumb idea overall to even think about trying alcohol. Curiosity got the best of me, and now my therapist, who was also my legal guardian, probably thought I was an alcoholic on top of being crazy. And the worst part? I was sixteen.

"Lana." I turned my head to see Trevor, now seated next to me on the sofa. "I want to apologize for the way I acted. I wasn't mad at you. It was personal stuff."

What kind of personal stuff was he referencing here?

"It's fine." I turned my attention back to the TV and continued watching my movie.

"I got you something." Slightly annoyed, I faced him again.

"Here." I watched in shock as he pulled out a little jewelry box and handed it to me.

"What's this?" I asked. "Just a little something from me to you." I opened the box to reveal a beautiful vintage bracelet encrusted with diamonds.

"What? Are these real diamonds?" I was taken by surprise when I could see my reflection in the little gemstones. "Real diamonds," he repeated.

I took the bracelet off my wrist and gently placed it back in the box. "Trevor, I can't accept this. This has to cost a couple thousand dollars at least."

He grinned. "Have you seen my house? Lana, I have millions. This little trinket doesn't even put a dent in my wallet." He grabbed the bracelet and slid it back on my wrist. I could easily conclude this was one of the nicest things I had ever owned. "Thank you," I whispered. "Seriously. It's beautiful."

The next week rolled around before I knew it, and I was slowly adjusting to this new routine. Today was supposed to mark my last therapy session with Trevor before he notified the police about my status.

They periodically called Trevor and asked how I was doing, considering how difficult I was throughout the whole process. This week consisted of questions, questions, and more questions. I tried my best to stay calm as I answered each of them.

It was 8:32 A.M., and I was wide awake. I was losing more and more sleep each day, but I was conditioned for this type of schedule by now.

"Good morning, Lana," said Trevor as he poured me a cup of coffee. This was also a part of my new morning routine.

Coffee was the only way my brain could stay awake through each dreaded therapy session. He handed me the freshly-brewed mug and went to find something to eat in the fridge.

"We will meet in the office when you're ready. I just have a few more questions for you today. Then I'll look through all my gathered info." I was praying all of this gathered info didn't lead to anything serious.

All of the information coming out of my mouth was nothing but the truth. How did he interpret all this? I had no idea, and I was a little scared of the possible explanations he could come up with.

Although it had been a full week, my heart wouldn't stop wondering when Salem was going to be back. Where was he now? For all I knew, he could be in a different city.

The cops were ruthlessly searching for him daily, but he was one step ahead of them. Regardless of whether he was still in Greenwood, or if he was halfway across the country, I knew the police were no match for Salem Coleman.

I wanted to give him a hug. Assure him that none of this was his fault. That he wasn't a bad person. "Alright, Lana. Let's head upstairs," said Trevor, who was now finished eating. I groaned.

This session was going to be the death of me, but at least I knew what to expect. Doing this ritual for a week straight made it easier for me to answer Trevor's questions comfortably.

I sat down in the same leather chair I had sat in countless times. Trevor faced me, pulled up his computer screen, and grabbed his notepad.

"Okay, Lana. So I've been studying you carefully based on your answers to my questions this week. I just need a few more questions before we end this session. For starters, why do you refuse to cooperate with the authorities for Salem Coleman's arrest?"

I gasped. "He's being arrested?"

Trevor glanced at his computer. "No, Lana. At least not yet. But if they were to arrest Salem, why would you refuse to cooperate with the authorities?"

Were we even on the same page?

"I feel like this is obvious. I wouldn't cooperate with authorities if they tried to arrest him because he would be getting falsely arrested." Trevor's pencil flew to the paper as he made his first note for today. "And you're telling me you do not like the police because they are trying to take Salem away from you?"

"I guess you could put it that way." All these questions were starting to sound the same.

"Why exactly do you care if Salem was out of the picture?"

"What do you mean by that? He's my best friend. Tell me, Trevor, how would you feel if your long term best friend was being arrested for something they didn't do?"

"Lana. We're talking about you, not me. I understand your frustration, but that's why we meet everyday. To sort these things out. To find out why you're frustrated.

These questions are provocative, but only because I need to dig deep into your mind, and find out how you would react depending on the manner."

I nodded. "Okay. I'm sorry."

"Don't be. Now let's continue. Lana, would you believe me if I told you that your life would be better if Salem was behind bars, where he couldn't harm you or hold you captive?"

"He's not holding me captive. He's never held me captive. Don't you understand? Being a psychiatrist, you should know based on my answers that I'm not lying to you. I'm sticking to the same storyline here. Why do you think I'm lying?" I said sharply.

"Actually, Lana, being a psychiatrist with almost thirty years of experience, a doctorate degree, and a medical degree, you're not the first patient to come from this situation. I've had lots of experience in this field and I don't want you to forget that."

"I don't understand. What are you trying to say here?"

"What I'm trying to tell you is that I don't necessarily think you're lying, per say. Although that word in itself is subjective, I think there's more to what you're trying to tell me, and the aroma I'm getting here is very clear."

"What *aroma* are you getting here?" I mocked. The more he spoke, the more confused I got.

"Listen, Lana. I don't want you to get all freaked out on me. But as a psychiatrist, it is my job to tell you these things. After heavily researching and comparing your case to many others I've had in the past, I think it is safe to conclude that -"

"Conclude what? What are you rambling about now?"

"Lana. Hear me out -"

"Why? You're freaking me out. What is it you're trying to say?" I stammered.

"Let me finish -"

"What is it?"

"Enough!" He yelled. "Lana, if you want to hear it in simple terms, you have *Stockholm Syndrome*." He dropped his pencil and let it roll off the table.

He slammed the door behind him as he exited, and left me there, in that room, to process something I didn't even want to consider.

"Stockholm Syndrome." I let it roll off my tongue. It didn't sound right. "*Stockholm Syndrome*." I said it again.
I'd briefly heard of it through an infamous news story a few years ago, and if I remember correctly, the case sounded insane. There was *no way* I had Stockholm Syndrome.

Where did Trevor go? I glanced at the notepad still sitting on his side of the desk. In bold letters at the bottom of all the notes he'd scribbled for days straight, read *Stockholm Syndrome*. Bright red pen, underlined.

I wanted to cry and scream into a pillow at the same time. But I did neither. I sat in that leather chair, unsure of what to do next.

I felt numb. My heart raced. I didn't have Stockholm Syndrome. Why would I have Stockholm Syndrome if I'd never been held captive? If I didn't have a captor to blame?

Salem was a rebellious player who committed countless crimes through his life at the orphanage and god knows where else. But he'd never in his life do something like that to someone. Especially not me.

Now that Trevor had pinned me as a victim of Stockholm Syndrome, I knew getting Salem out of this was going to be much harder. If they really thought I had Stockholm Syndrome, they wouldn't count a word I said with the credentials they deserved.

What would Phoebe think? What would Phoebe do in my situation? It'd been a long time since I saw her face.

It felt like the world was against me. Like it was trying to mock me, and taunt me relentlessly. For what? I didn't deserve this. Why couldn't I have just been born into a normal life?

Instead, I was left with the burden of things I couldn't even process. I stood up from the chair, feeling weak at my knees, so I could go look for Trevor. Ask him what to do next, because clearly I had no idea.

"Trevor," I mumbled as I headed downstairs. I saw him shuffling more newspapers in the kitchen. He stuffed them back into a drawer and eyed me.

"Listen, Lana. I'm sorry, okay? I know it's my job as your psychiatrist to help you. Instead, I lost my patience and reacted immaturely. I know you're probably mad, but we can't let that get in the way of your treatment. Can we continue with this?"

I could hear the sincerity in his voice, and I forgave him. After all, he was the only person present in my life right now. What good would it bring if I stayed mad at him?

"Okay," I said.

We headed back upstairs in the small office. "Trevor, I know you're the psychiatrist here," I said as I sat down. "But you should know I don't have Stockholm Syndrome. Believe me or don't believe me, I don't really care. But you can't throw something like this at me. Salem doesn't deserve to go to prison. Do you know what this could do to him?" I whined.

"Lana, I know this is a lot to take in. But your brain is just reacting this way because you don't want to accept this fact. Do you even know what Stockholm Syndrome is?" He asked.

I nodded with confidence. "I know exactly what it is, and I don't have it. I also know that my brain isn't reacting this way just because I'm freaked out. Maybe I am freaked out, but not because I have Stockholm Syndrome. It's because I know I *don't* have it and don't really know how to tell you that."

He sighed. "You're a smart girl. I'm sure you know that. But it is the best logical explanation here. When the cops were called to take you to safety, you were reluctant." He overemphasized that last word. "This is a common sign with victims facing Stockholm Syndrome. Have you ever let a bird out of its cage? When a bird has been in that cage for so long, it might stay in that little cage despite having the opportunity to flee because it is in *denial*."

I gasped. "You think I'm in denial here? I can't believe you people. I'm not in denial!" I yelled.

Trevor flipped to a new page in his notepad and wrote everything down. "Of course you wouldn't think you're in denial," Trevor laughed. "That's the whole meaning of being in denial. It's when you refuse to accept the extent of reality because it's too much for you to handle. You don't know how to react to the situation, and that's why you need me."

"I know you're trying to help, but I'm trying to tell you that you're wasting your time by doing all this. I don't have Stockholm Syndrome, and you can't tell me otherwise. If you really wanted to help me, you'd ignore the cops and help me find my friend so we could run away from all this."

"Lana, my job here is not to convince you, or try to make you feel a certain way. My job is however, to give you the proper diagnosis so we can move on. I didn't spend a decade studying psychology and the human mind for nothing, you know." He chuckled.

"I've dealt with this before, and I've helped so many people," he continued. "Whether you choose to accept this diagnosis or not, we're going to fix you."

I sighed. I felt defeated. There wasn't much I could do to get Trevor to hear me out.

At the end of the day, I was the only one on this planet besides Salem who knew what our friendship was like, and what really happened on the day of my disappearance. Trevor might've been a licensed professional, but that didn't automatically mean he was qualified to write my life story. I loved and respected him for what he was trying to do for me, but it wasn't what I needed.

Could I really blame him? My case was pretty complicated because of Salem's devious past and our odd friendship. He probably was convinced I was a victim of this phenomenon, but only I knew this was so far from the truth.

All I wanted to do was go outside and flush out my problems by absorbing some sunlight and fresh air, but I couldn't even do that. Why did it matter so much if I stayed inside? Nothing bad was to come if I stepped out the front door, but I was overruled by that argument too.

There was no room to even complain about my circumstances, because right then and there, Trevor was already giving me a history lesson on Stockholm Syndrome. I briefly learned about it, but my education wasn't exactly ideal.

"So you see, Lana," Trevor rambled, "in 1973, Sweden was met with a man who fired shots into the ceiling of a bustling bank. The man took four of the bank employees and held them hostage. Throughout their captivity in a bank vault, the man formed a peculiar bond with his victims by showing them acts of kindness and trust when they needed it." I paid my full attention to him, because I was actually kind of fascinated. But no way did I relate to anything he was saying.

"When given the opportunity to escape, the hostages weren't supportive of the idea. In fact, they built such a relationship with their captor, they despised the police and anyone who was trying to part them from the man who put them in this situation to begin with."

I adopted what he was saying quite easily, because it truly was an unexplainable phenomenon that some people actually had to suffer. But I was not one of them. In fact, I was no victim at all.

"Some examples of this tricky mentality can vary, but here are a few to consider. For instance, if a person develops Stockholm Syndrome after a year of befriending their captor, it most likely won't phase them if their captor poses the threat that they will kill a friend. In the victim's mind, they are simply grateful that the captor wasn't threatening to kill *them*. It sounds terrible in a sane person's mind, but this is just the brain's response in terms of enduring this form of abuse for so long."

He was right about that. In a sane person's mind, that sounds crazy. I was that sane person. I, Lana, also known as the girl with Stockholm Syndrome, thought that sounded insane.

"Thanks for educating me on Stockholm Syndrome. But I can't relate to anything you're saying here. Salem never posed any threats to me or anyone I knew."

"Sure you could. You might not admit it, but sometimes, captors use more subtle ways to pose a threat. Maybe you haven't noticed, but clearly there's something telling me that you are rebelling against the police and helping Salem because he is holding a power against you. You have to understand, he doesn't have that power anymore."

I groaned. "He never had a power against me. He never forced me to do anything I wasn't comfortable with."

Just as I said that, flashbacks were pouring through my mind of that horrid night at the bar. The bar he dragged me to, even though I had made it clear I did not want to associate with alcohol.

But that was different. He didn't force me. He begged me, and being his best friend who also didn't want him to get into any trouble, I tagged along. My point still stood firm. He had a big heart, and people overlooked that because he didn't talk about his personal life unless he was positive he could trust you with it.

After what seemed like hours of my day wasted, our therapy session was finally over. Trevor tried his best to persuade me that my case fit those who actually suffered from Stockholm Syndrome, but I didn't believe him.

All throughout his words, I was imagining all the nice things Salem had done for me. He cared for me like I was his little sister, not his hostage. Just putting it that way made me want to puke. When would I get it through to the cops and Trevor that Salem wasn't a criminal? Not soon enough, that was for sure. But soon.

Chapter 15:

It was midnight, and I couldn't get any sleep. Part of me was telling me I should listen to Trevor and his theory, but there was no chance of that happening.

It was crazy how words could warp how you see yourself so easily. I saw myself as a strong girl who could get through anything, but other people saw me as a poor little orphan girl who was now the victim of Stockholm Syndrome. And when I say they, I'm talking about Trevor, the police, and whoever else was going to see my story once it appeared on the news.

I sat in the empty bedroom, staring at the covered window that hid the outside. I wanted more than anything to crawl out of it and have some time to myself. Maybe even try to find Salem, or at the very least, some answers. But for some reason, I couldn't bring myself to do it.

I could get in serious trouble with the police if I attempted to run out on my own, but that's when I decided it would be worth it. I told myself it wasn't a big deal, as I'd be back before the sun came up.

I waited about an hour to be sure Trevor was asleep before making my move.

I had never actually been in his bedroom before, and today was not going to be the day to see it for the first time. I carried on with my plan and realized it was now time to find a window that was easy to climb out of.

I checked each hallway before deciding to use the front door.

I carefully unlocked the beautifully crafted door and bolted as soon as it swung open. I knew as long as I got home soon enough, no one would suspect a thing. As my sandals slapped against the pavement and the wind whipped my auburn hair back, I found myself temporarily free from my problems.

It felt so good to be wandering the empty streets of Greenwood. And that's when I found myself wondering, was this what Salem had been doing? Walking around in the dead of night on the lookout for police?

I felt a wave of sadness rush over me, and suddenly, tears were streaking my cheeks. I wiped them away with my sleeve and continued walking, this time slower.

I felt horrible that I had led him to run away like this. He had done this countless times while he was at the orphanage, but this was far more serious. I made my way into a typically-crowded area where shops and restaurants stood. It kind of reminded me of North Augusta, my hometown.

I sat down on a bench and reminisced on all the events I could remember when we had first left the orphanage. That day we grabbed lemonades, my little episode in the alleyway, room 212 in that little beat up motel.

When we first grabbed water bottles from that gas station down the street; that day we went swimming in the community pool. *That day.* Why did it end strangely again?

Right. That man, who recognized me while Salem and I were swimming. The anonymous caller who gave tips to the police - *him.*

The man with the yellow canary tattoo on his neck - if it was anyone, it had to be him.

Whatever his name was, or whoever he was. He had to have called the police and tipped them on the situation. Maybe I was onto something here.

What did he look like again? The only thing that came to mind when I thought of him was the canary tattoo and his streaky blonde hair.

Why did he call in now, when he saw me a few months ago? Did he think he was saving me by tipping the police or something? Did he lead the police here?

How did he know so much to direct the police to the orphanage I ran away from? I stood up from the bench and brushed off my pants. Time to continue walking.

I breathed heavily as I inhaled the cold weather. The cold, dry air stung my lungs.

Where would Salem be? The bar? I'd give anything to tell him exactly what was happening with the police. I wanted to go check the nightclub he had taken me to the other week, but I had no idea how to get there. What if he was long gone? Or worse - what if he did something bad to himself? No. He wasn't *that* stranded.

I tried to ignore the bad thoughts swirling through my mind, but I couldn't. They stayed there, and they weren't going anywhere.

I checked the bulletin board I had been to a few weeks ago to see if there were still any *Missing Persons* posters. I guess the police had taken them all down after finding me safe. Any updates on the murdered women?

I skimmed through all the clippings, ads, and posters to find out, but instead, I came across something worse. Was my mind playing tricks on me? I rubbed my eyes and snatched the poster off the wall.

"WANTED" was sprawled at the top, and there was Salem's picture on the cover. A $2,000 reward was being issued out to anyone who could find him, or lead the police to him. They couldn't be serious.

I held the poster with trembling hands and tried to study it. There had to be more posters like this out there. Maybe Trevor was right when he said I was in denial, because I refused to accept the fact that they were convinced Salem Coleman had kidnapped me.

I was relieved they didn't specify what he was wanted for, because that would've made me even more infuriated.

Holding this poster made me want to protect Salem even more than I already had. He didn't deserve to have his face plastered all over "WANTED" ad clippings.

I looked around to see if anyone else was present, but no one was in sight. I was happy about that, because I was pretty sure I looked like I had just come out of jail myself. I wiped away any more tears still on my face and led myself away from the bulletin board.

I should've been home by now, but with the poster still in hand, I couldn't bring myself to head back to Trevor's just yet. Instead, I walked around the city to find more of these posters so I could take them down if I found them. The less posters, the better, was what I kept assuring myself.

I had circled around this area, looking for more newspaper clippings or bulletin boards. I had racked up three "WANTED" posters with Salem on the cover and observed them all. I didn't plan on keeping them. Wouldn't seeing them just make me feel worse?

I decided to keep one of them in case I needed it for whatever reason, and with rage still burning in me, I crumpled up the other two and threw them away. Forget real therapy. This was the kind of therapy I needed to stay grounded.

I headed back to Trevor's feeling numb and now cold. I folded up the poster.

Trevor seeing the poster in my hands would show him I left the house. Going to sleep was the best thing for me right now. The bags under my eyes weren't getting any lighter, and neither was the weight on my shoulders. Salem Coleman, *where are you?*

When I got to Trevor's, I stepped onto the polished patio and overlooked the mansion that I temporarily called home.

When Salem and I reunite, I plan to start my own life; finally live the way I always wanted. Maybe finish highschool, and go to college.

I wasn't sure what Salem had in mind for his future, but to be honest, he probably had no idea. That was okay though. Because I knew what I wanted and we were dependent on each other.

The poster was still in my hand, and I had a tight grip on it. I didn't want anyone else to see it, as the less people saw his picture, the safer he'd be.

I tried to open the front door, but realized stupidly I had locked it on my way out. I guess I didn't really think this through.

There were tons of windows around the house, but only a few of them were unlocked. I had to play my cards right so Trevor didn't catch me. I could feel the tension and embarrassment building up already.

I checked each window for a lock. Most of them weren't budging, but I guess luck was on my side that day, because there was an unlocked window on the first floor. I climbed through carefully and slid inside.

I was now in the living room. I closed the window and locked it to avoid any suspicion, and finally, I was staring at the giant TV in Trevor's house.

It felt good in a way to be rebellious. Maybe that's why Salem did it. The thrill of sneaking out without a real motive made my adrenaline spike, and I liked the rush it gave me.

I couldn't wait to tell Salem everything. About how I snuck out and explored the city at night. About how I discreetly took down all of his "WANTED" posters. But would I ever get to tell him? I had my hopes, and I wasn't letting them go just yet. He could be anywhere, for all I knew. But what if he was *dead*?

I hated saying that, because it was so unlikely. The words *he* and *dead* combined in the same sentence made me shiver. It was a thought I kept in the back of my head. But all these thoughts were eating my insides raw.

I made it into our bedroom and climbed in bed. The teddy bear Salem had won for me had taken his place. The covers were ruffled, and they stayed in the same position Salem had left them in the night he was drunk.

I couldn't tell whether I wanted to hug the bear tightly or rip its head off. The memory of us at the arcade having a blast made me both happy and depressed knowing I'd never relive that night again.

I remembered the last few nights with Salem. When I had helped him upstairs because he was buzzed. It was funny looking back at how out of it he was, but it wasn't funny anymore. What if he was doing that every night? Only, he wouldn't have someone else to help him. What if he was smoking a whole pack of cigarettes everyday? What if he was getting into constant bar fights with gang members? What if he *himself* had joined a gang? Oh my god. Could he actually be in a *gang*?

I wasn't there to keep him out of trouble. I wish I was. What if he had overdosed on some sort of crazy drug? Marijuana. Bath Salts. Acid. Cocaine. The list went on and on.

There were so many possibilities. My head hurt just thinking about all those possibilities. I tossed and turned, trying to ignore all the horrible thoughts that something bad already happened to him. Hit by a car on his way out of a nightclub. Sleeping on a bench every night with nothing but the clothes on his back. Stealing from gas stations to eat since he blew all of his cash on booze. I shuddered.

Sometimes your brain could be your best friend. The one to get you an A+ on an algebra test. The one to help you remember your uncle's birthday. But other times, it could be your worst enemy. The thing that was holding you back from pursuing your dreams. The thing that presumed your sister dead because she didn't reply to your text from last night. The thing that forced you to starve yourself so you could drop ten pounds.

Everyone's brain was different, but they all had one thing in common.

They all had the power to send us into a downward spiral. Some people unfortunately couldn't get out of that spiral. And I think I was officially slipping.

Chapter 16:

"You okay?"

I finally jolted awake after the third time he called my name. "Hi," I muttered as I climbed out of bed.

"Good morning. Are you okay?" He repeated.

I glanced at my body and frowned. "I think so. Why?" He laughed. "You weren't waking up very easily."

I shrugged it off. The last thing I remembered was falling asleep at five in the morning. My brain wouldn't let me rest until then. It was now eight in the morning, and I already knew why Trevor had woken me up.

"I don't want to," I groused.

"Lana, it's therapy. The police are already aware of your condition. You can't just ignore your treatment." He was holding two cups of coffee and handed one to me.

"This doesn't make me want to do more counseling." My eyes were fixated on the mug before taking a sip. The hot coffee burned the roof of my mouth when I drank it, but I just tried to ignore it.

Trevor sat down next to me on the bed and put his hand on my shoulder. "You know what? Let's go somewhere."

Confused, I gave him the side eye. "Where?"

He smiled. "Follow me to the car. It's a surprise." I sighed. I didn't have the motivation to go anywhere, but it would've required more energy to object, and I was pretty low on that stuff.

If we operated on batteries, I was pretty convinced I'd be dead already. Trying not to look as miserable as I really was, I stood up from the bed and followed Trevor to the front door.

My legs were slightly wobbly and I was struggling to keep my eyes open.

Trevor shut the car door as I settled into the leather seat. I coughed up the energy to fasten my seatbelt and tried my hardest not to close my eyes. It felt like if I closed them, they'd never open again. And so I tried to fight the weights of my eyelids for the rest of the ride.

It was so hard paying attention to Trevor when all I could do was stare out the window. All I saw was the occasional person and their dog, or sidewalks or pine trees; but all I really hoped to see was Salem. I didn't care where, or what he was doing. I just wanted to see him somewhere.

"We're here," Trevor said cheerily. I came back to my senses and took off my seatbelt.

"A mall?" I asked suspiciously. Trevor never seemed like the person to shop at traditional outlets like these. "Of course," he said. "Come on. Let's go shopping."

I walked into the mall and observed all the other girls shopping with their friends. They giggled and twirled their hair as they held their shopping bags to various boutiques and jewelry shops.

I felt the slightest bit of envy as I walked past girls like these, but the envy would subside as I crossed paths with other people, such as old couples or guys and their friends.

I guess I was just jealous that I was spending my teenage years as a sixteen-year-old girl like this. Being neglected at an orphanage. Being derived from my friends. Well, my friend. If Salem and I were here with each other, I'd probably be having a blast right now. Or maybe even Phoebe, despite her distaste for cliques like those.

Instead, I was now walking with a rich man who was slightly balding and had the coldest blue eyes you'd ever see.

Of course, I wasn't complaining. He did have wealth and a stable job. And a heart of gold. Or at least silver. But he still wasn't my father. He was my therapist, and I didn't see that changing anytime soon. Or ever.

"So . . . why are we here exactly?" I asked Trevor.

"We're here for you, Lana! Clearly I'm not looking to buy anything. I've got everything I need." He winked with a smile. "For me?" He nodded.

Then suddenly he got more serious. "Technically, you're supposed to be inside right now. Don't put yourself out there too much. We'll head back home when you're ready," he whispered. He was probably expecting a grin from me, or at the very least, a reaction. But I just blankly stared at him. "We can head home now if you're not going to buy anything," I said.

His expression dampened a little after I said that. "You can buy anything you want. We can go to every single store in this mall if we have to. Sound fun?" He exclaimed.

I shrugged. "Just get me a burrito and a Coke. Then we can get out of here."

Trevor shook his head. "Don't you understand? You could buy fancy diamond necklaces, giant TVs, designer clothing, funky socks. I don't care. I've got plenty of cash." He whipped out a fat stack of cash and briefly waved it around before stuffing it back into his wallet.

Three weeks ago, I would've probably freaked out after hearing I could buy anything I wanted in a shopping mall. But not even a million dollars could replace the bond I had with my best friend.

"I don't want shiny necklaces or funky socks. We can leave now."

Trevor sighed heavily. "Wow. You sure are tired, huh?" *More than he'd ever know.*

"Come on, Lana. There's gotta be one thing in this whole mall you would want." I nodded. "Sure thing. I know exactly what I want."

His eyes lit up and he watched as I headed towards a vending machine and paid for an energy drink with the bit of cash I had in my pocket. The energy drink fell into the slot with a thud and I reached down to grab it. "Done." I watched as his expression fell again.

"I could've paid for that," he told me. "I know."

"I just don't understand," he mumbled. "I'm practically waving hundred-dollar bills in your face. There's gotta be one thing in this mall you want to buy. I don't care how much it costs." He gestured towards all the different stores we were surrounded by. From jewelry shops, to toy stores, the options were endless. But chugging the can of energy in my hands was enough to make me feel a little less weary.

Trevor practically dragged me into a beauty store. "You like this stuff, right?" He asked as he frantically looked around the aisles of makeup.

He grabbed a shopping basket and handed it to me. "Wow! Whatever this stuff is, here you go." He tossed an expensive tube of mascara in my basket. "And this stuff! Whatever this is." In went a bottle of foundation. It wasn't even close to my shade.

"Ooh, Lana. Look at this!" He grabbed a colorful eyeshadow pallet and handed it to me. "It has all the colors of the rainbow. Whatever it does." He dashed to another aisle and grabbed a few lipsticks off a shelf. The people in the store were now looking at him like he was crazy.

"Okay, Trevor. That's enough." He gave me a pleading look. "Smile. Please." I faked a smile and let my face drop again. "Please tell me why you're upset."

I rolled my eyes. "I appreciate your efforts, Trevor. I really do. But right now I'm trying to cope with losing Salem. I mean, he's probably dead right now, and I can't -" my voice trailed off. I realized I was just repeating what kept me up at night out loud. I caught myself before I kept going.

"I just miss him, and all this fancy makeup isn't going to change that. Sorry." I reached to put all of the items in the basket away, but he grabbed it before me. "I got it," he said. I could tell he was disappointed, but could you blame me? I swallowed my emotions and tried my best not to let my eyes water.

I finished off the whole can of the energy drink in the car. I could've gotten anything I possibly wanted, with a rich guy supplying me all this money. But I simply refused.

You might think I was crazy. Hell, the old me stuck in the orphanage would've thought I was insane. But the mental state I had reached drove me to stop caring. To stop putting an effort into what I wore. Into whether or not I had brushed my hair that morning. Did it really matter? I found myself challenging this exact statement everyday now. When you finally hit rock bottom and look up at the sky, it just seems so far away. My energy was diluted, if there was any left.

I wasn't sure why Trevor cared so much. Did he feel bad that I was a "victim" of Stockholm Syndrome? Clearly I wasn't, but when a psychiatrist with so much knowledge to give had labeled me with such a name, there was only so much I could say to convince him otherwise.

It's funny how much of an imprint one person can leave in your mind. When they leave abruptly, whether or not it was their choice, it could drive you mental. At least, that was the best way I could put it. It felt like a part of me had died. Because maybe Salem really had died.

The police didn't care. They thought he was a malicious criminal who deserved nothing.

But I saw him for who he really was. He left such a deep imprint in my mind that I started believing I couldn't even step outside without him. Could I? Maybe not. Maybe I was just mental for *him*.

We pulled into Trevor's driveway. The whole ride had been silent, but it's not like I had the energy to talk much anyway.

"I tried," Trevor said, now rhythmically tapping his steering wheel. He pulled the keys out of the ignition and opened the door, flashing me a cold glance in the rear view mirror. "Therapy."

Chapter 17:

I anxiously trudged to the front door without question.

I guess he was right. He did try to make me feel better, but if he knew anything about me, he'd know that once I was down, it would take everything to get me back on my feet.

Speaking of my feet, they were killing me. Every bone in my body ached. Did this mean I really was spiraling? If this was how I felt, I didn't even want to imagine what Salem was dealing with right now. If he was even alive, which I was really starting to doubt.

I tried to steady my breathing before I stepped into the office for my dumb therapy session.

I guess you couldn't really argue with someone who knew twice as much as you did. Trevor was a genius, and there was no denying it. All of his certificates and awards adorning the narrow hallways spoke for themselves. As you made your way through his beautiful lavished home, they all stuck out like trophies.

Would I be staying in Trevor's house forever? Probably not. But when this was all over, where would I go? Regardless of whether Salem was dead or went to jail, I'd be stuck.

I went into the kitchen to throw away the now empty energy drink. Weren't these things really bad for you? I looked on the back of the can out of curiosity and yawned when I saw the sugar contents. I couldn't be bothered with my health anymore. If I was "suffering" from Stockholm Syndrome, a little extra sugar and insomnia wouldn't hurt.

At sixteen, I should already know what I wanted to do with my life. Shouldn't Trevor be discussing these things with me because he was a therapist? In all honesty, I didn't think his help would even matter because I'd still be clueless. Whether I chose to accept it or not was a different story. But was it really? I had already come to terms with my fate. Suddenly, the police didn't look so scary anymore.

"Let's just get this over with." I slouched into the leather chair and tried not to make direct eye contact. Doing that would just make me more uncomfortable than I already was.

"Hi, Lana. So, for today's session, I want to introduce something to you I haven't yet mentioned." I nodded. "Go on."

He cleared his throat. "I feel like we've gone enough in depth on the cause of your mental disorder, but we haven't actually started your treatment yet. I want to go over this with you so we are on the same page. Have you ever heard of a treatment method called psychotherapy?"

I shook my head, unable to absorb what he was telling me. "Nope."

He laughed nervously. "Well, it's something I like to call 'talking therapy'. This is an excellent way to help subdue the mental traumas you've experienced. It sounds scarier than it really is." As if I cared.

"Anyways, this process is going to take a lot of patience and tolerance from us both in order to be carried through successfully. Understand?"

"Sure," was all I could bring myself to say. Because it wasn't worth fighting over, even if I didn't understand what the hell he was talking about.

"Great. Now, one of the many goals in psychotherapy is for the two of us to have a trusted relationship with each other. As your therapist, I make it a priority of mine to build a mutual trust with you so you feel comfortable with my help." He paused to make sure I was keeping up. I wasn't.

"Another goal of mine is by the end of your treatment to enable your mind to its full potential." He overemphasized that last word.

I think he had a habit of overenthusiasm. Not sure if that was a good or bad thing, judging from my facial expression. Here's a hint, I wasn't smiling.

"But first, let's do a little warm up." He pulled out a canvas and some markers from a desk drawer and placed them in front of me.

I stared at the blank canvas unamused. "You want me to color?"

He shook his head. "I want you to draw the person you love the most."

I furrowed my brow. How was this supposed to help me?

He brushed his hand against mine, grazing the diamond encrusted bracelet he initially placed on my wrist. I tried not to look so fazed as he smiled, but the whole encounter was really bizarre.

"Start drawing," he told me, and then stood up from his chair. "I'll give you some time to yourself to finish."

As soon as he left the room, I picked up the pens and started drawing.

I was no artist, but using all the colorful markers, I was able to make a rough doodle of Salem and his dark brown hair.

I wasn't totally sure he was the person I loved the most in my whole life, but with him being gone and all, he was the only person that came to my mind.

When Trevor reentered the room, I put the markers down and picked up my canvas.

"Let's see who you drew," he said enthusiastically. I held up the canvas for him to see, but when he did, his whole expression went from excited to annoyed.

"Who's that?" He finally said.

"Salem," I said wearily. I thought it was pretty obvious.

He cleared his throat. "Right," he assured. "You can't think of anyone *else* that's made an impact on your life recently?"

I shrugged. "My grandma, but she passed away a few years ago."

Trevor seemingly waited for me to continue, but I didn't.

"Alright; well, now that the warm up is over with, let's get straight to your treatment." He grabbed the canvas from my hands and chucked it into the trash can behind his chair.

I could've sworn I heard him mutter something about me needing a lot of therapy to *fix this mess,* but I just ignored him.

It had taken more than an hour for my therapy session to finally finish, but when it was over, I did not hesitate to rush out of the office.

Here I was, bored, but just relieved that weird ordeal was over. What now?

I had been doing the same things for the past few weeks - reading old books, rereading them, watching movies, eating, and sleeping. Sometimes I'd have a detailed conversation with Trevor over the dumbest things, but at least it helped me cope with the fact that I'd never cross paths with Salem again.

There was only so much I could do when I was stuck indoors, but this house was far from ordinary. There were so many rooms I had yet to explore, and considering Trevor was busy scheduling future appointments with his actual mentally-ill clients, I took it upon myself to venture out.

I walked down a long hallway and was now facing several closed doors. Peeking in each of them wouldn't do any harm, right? I opened the first door to my left and peered through the crack.

Inside was another bare office with a few chairs, a nice desk, and more certificates. The usual for all his offices. Why did he need so many?

I assumed it was because he deals with a lot of patients during the day, and works long hours from home at night. I carried on down the hall and opened the next door.

This time, I was feeling more bold than before. I stepped inside the next room, which was surprisingly big. Inside was a pool table, a foosball table, and neat vintage wall art touching up the atmosphere of the room. A man cave?

There were collectible bottles and beer caps displayed on shelves, and there was even a mini fridge and a bar in the corner that was now covered in dust.

Why hadn't he told me about any of these rooms? Or specifically, this one? I loved it in here, and while I wanted to stick around, I kept walking to the next room, carefully shutting the door behind me.

I figured it'd be better to ask Trevor later if he wanted to play pool with me.

I hadn't touched a cue stick in years. I wondered if Salem played pool. I'm sure he has. He used to sneak out of the orphanage late at night to do whatever he wanted on the streets, and I'm sure he's been to plenty of bars before that had pool tables. How much fun he probably had - *enough about Salem.* He was either living under a different name on the other side of the country or long gone.

It was time to sneak into the next room. I had high hopes for this one, considering I had just discovered a literal man cave in the last one.

I pushed the door open. This one took a lot of arm strength to push, because it seemed like the lock on the door had been altered. But when I finally opened it, my eyes grew wide.

The room was small, and dark. There were several different bulletin boards marked with masking tape and newspaper clippings of the recent murders of the three women in Greenwood. Woah. I was already amazed that this dude was a psychiatrist. Was he some sort of private detective too?

I slowly approached the desk with the bulletin boards above it. I studied each newspaper clipping carefully- there were lots of paper clues overlapping each other. There were all sorts of cool stuff in this room- abnormal bookshelves filled with books about criminals and their everyday thoughts.

A filing cabinet stood in the far corner, and I had the sudden urge to open the drawers.

All three drawers were locked. Weird. Perhaps some private files or contracts? Curiosity got the best of me, and I snooped around until I discovered a little silver key sitting on the desk. I wiggled the key into the first lock, and sure enough, the drawer slid open.

I rummaged through the junk inside of the drawer and didn't find anything too interesting. A magnifying glass was probably the coolest thing I could find in the compartment.

The second drawer was fairly similar, but as I dug through its contents, I found an old birthday card addressed to Trevor. It looked to be a handmade card, with the picture of a teddy bear crafted on the cover.

As I opened the card, an old stained Polaroid picture fell into my lap. What's this?

It looked to be a younger version of Trevor, with less gray hairs and a darker beard. It was a picture of Trevor and a woman hugging each other while smiling at the camera. Cute, I thought. I set down the Polaroid and read the note inside the card. It read:

Happy Birthday, Trevor! I can't believe you're already 49. Don't forget to have lots of fun on this special day. Sending you lots of love! Sincerely, Debbie

I shook it off. It must've been an old card from a friend. This card had to have been at least five years old. There was no real date on the card anywhere, but clearly whoever wrote the card wasn't in Trevor's life anymore. I set it aside and opened the last drawer.

It took a few minutes, but after tugging vigorously on the drawer and digging into the lock with the key, it opened enough for me to see a gun and a wallet sitting alone. Why did Trevor have a gun?

I didn't touch it, as I wanted nothing to do with anything dangerous. It could've easily been loaded, and I wasn't willing to check.

But the wallet - it was so out of place. The leather was now ripping on the cover and the wallet didn't have a metal clasp or button to secure it with. What if there was money inside? Or cool spy tools?

I was pretty excited, if you couldn't already tell. But instead of movie-type spy gadgets and wads of cash, a few ID cards fell out. Fake IDs? Were they Trevor's? I had so many questions already.

I picked up the first ID card. This ID belonged to a woman named Felicia. Wait a minute. *Felicia White?* I read the name over and over again.

Instantly, my mind flashed back to the newspaper I saw when I first arrived at Greenwood. Was this just a twisted coincidence?

The picture on the ID was of a woman who looked like Felicia's picture on the newspaper. Why would he have this if she was dead?

Everything was accurate. There was no denying that this ID was authentic. This was weird. As in, disturbing weird. I dropped the ID back onto the floor with a perplexed look on my face and picked up the next one.

I was a little scared to read the name, but my eyes eventually focused on it. *Serenity Hall.* As in, Serenity who was murdered a few weeks ago.

Serenity wasn't the most common name. Anybody could tell you that. I was starting to think this was more than just a coincidence.

Serenity's picture was genuine. She had a faint smile on her face that was hard to forget. That same smile was in her newspaper. And the dimples - they were there, just like the photo I could remember from the ad. This couldn't be, right? I set down the card and picked up the third.

Deborah Stallard was the owner of this one. I paused. Deborah. *Debbie.*

This was all starting to make sense. This card belonged to Debbie the pharmacist. I glanced back over to the birthday card still sitting on the floor where I had left it. *Sincerely, Debbie.*

Could this mean Debbie, the woman who was killed, wrote this card? Maybe it was a different Debbie. But there was no way this was some stupid coincidence. Why would a psychiatrist need the IDs of murdered victims? It's not like he counseled dead people. This was all too much. Could this mean? *No.* I didn't want to believe it.

The man who had so much love and patience to give to other people might not be the person everybody thinks he is. Trevor

MacQuoid - the rich, famous psychiatrist everyone raved about in this city - could be more than just a doctor with a heart of gold.

He was no secret detective that studied criminals. He *was* the criminal. But not just any criminal - a serial killer. A capital crime. One that could throw you in federal prison to rot for the rest of your life. That, or a death sentence.

I couldn't picture someone like my own therapist and now legal guardian being in shackles. But with every piece contributing to the puzzle now being solved in my brain, maybe I really could see him in shackles and even an orange jumpsuit. I shuddered.

Staring into the eyes of Debbie's picture knowing she was no longer alive sent chills down my spine. That was almost all of the ID cards, but there was one left. I didn't even want to pick this one up. The last three cards all belonged to murder victims. Which one could this be?

I reluctantly grabbed it off the floor and stared at it. I felt paralyzed. Like I had just been zapped with a lightning bolt. But this was no lightning bolt. This was reality. Staring back at me was my own picture. This very ID I was now holding had my own picture on it.

There was my name, neatly printed at the top. No one could miss that name, especially not me. After all, it was my name. My hands were now shaking and I broke into a cold sweat. I was already horrified at the thought that Trevor might be a deranged murderer, but the thought of me being his next victim never crossed my mind as a possibility until now.

I wanted to scream and cry both at the same time, but I could do neither. I just stood there, dumbfounded. That lightning bolt sure was seizing.

I felt like throwing up. Throwing up all my problems sure sounded good right now. Anything to get them out of my system. But unfortunately, it didn't work that way. I couldn't let go of my ID card. I held onto it and just stared blankly.

I guess I had lost track of time, or maybe my hearing decided to stop working completely, because the next thing I knew, hands were clamped on my neck.

These hands surely weren't being gentle, either. They slowly pressed harder and harder into my throat until I couldn't breathe anymore.

I coughed and tried to inhale some form of oxygen so I wouldn't pass out, but he had such a strong grip on my neck, I knew breathing was impossible at this point.

I tried prying his hands off with my own, but that was no use. He was too strong, and I had practically starved myself for the whole day because of my battle with depression. That didn't help my case very much.

I tried to scream, but nothing came out. I wriggled and tossed myself around in attempts to save myself, but his hands were closing tighter and tighter on my neck. My vision was starting to blur, and all I could hear now was Trevor yelling, "Fuck." Did he realize what he was doing?

People didn't just go around strangling others for fun, you know. He knew exactly what he was doing. And I couldn't believe it.

I wanted to beg for my life, tell him I wanted to go to college when I turned eighteen. Tell him about just wanting acceptance. I wanted so badly to tell him why I needed my life. I could already imagine my face on the cover of a newspaper. I had always wanted to become famous, like any other teenage girl. But being famous because you were murdered wasn't exactly something I wanted to be remembered for.

I gagged and my head started to throb. My voice was hoarse, and you could barely hear the words I was trying to say. "Stop" was all I could choke out, but it's not like anyone could hear me. Was I really dying?

With how long I had been fighting for my life, I was surprised I wasn't dead yet. Asphyxiation was going to be the slow, painful death of me. I had practically accepted my fate and let my hands drop limply when the door suddenly burst open.

"Get the hell off her!" was all I could hear. And it was right then and there that I had realized that my best friend who drove me to depression was not dead. That he was very much alive, and well. Salem Coleman - my alleged captor that led me to undergo therapy - was now battering my therapist.

I couldn't see Salem or Trevor, because they were both behind me. Trevor's hands were not letting go, and I still couldn't breathe. It was as if things were now happening in slow motion.

I wanted so badly to cry and run up to him. Let him know how grateful I was that he had miraculously appeared to save my life. But I was still in Trevor's grasp, and Salem started throwing punches and even kicking Trevor in attempts to knock him over. Or maybe he was trying to knock him out - I couldn't exactly tell.

Salem finally punched Trevor in the face. I couldn't actually see it happen, but that was probably a good thing. I didn't like seeing violence or anything of the sort, but in this case, violence was necessary, and I think Salem finally realized that. Another blow to the face, and I was pretty convinced Trevor's teeth were knocked out by now.

That did it. My neck was free from his grasp.

I crashed to the floor and took the biggest gasp of air I'd ever taken. At last it felt like I would actually survive. Despite being weak and now struggling to sit upright, I watched as Salem continued beating Trevor.

It hurt to watch, but I knew he deserved it. He was a murderer, and I was about to become a real victim. Not for being kidnapped, or having Stockholm Syndrome, but for being strangled to death.

The thought made my heart sink, but it felt good just to say that my heart was still working. God only knows what would've happened if Salem hadn't come to fight off Trevor in the time that he did. *Wait a minute*. Why was he here?

I snapped back to reality to see Trevor was now probably on the brink of death. "Okay, stop!" I called out to Salem. "You'll kill the guy!"

That didn't sound like the worst thing in the world right now, but deep down I knew that I would never be able to live with myself knowing Salem actually killed someone for me. Even if it was my attacker.

He let Trevor go before locking eyes with me for the first time. Trevor fell to the ground, and I took a good look at his face. His eyes were bruised, and his face was swollen and red from the punches he had just taken to the face. His nose was bleeding, and drops of blood were now all over the floor. I felt remorse for him, despite the fact that he had just tried to kill me.

I looked back at Salem, tears in my eyes. I tried to stand on my two feet, but collapsed back to the floor. He rushed over to me in a panic and helped me sit up in a comfortable position.

"Don't move," he said. "Hang in there, Lana. Are you okay? Can you see me clearly?"

Still feeling dazed, I found it hard to understand him. But I simply nodded and tried to keep my head from falling.

"Why did he have his hands on you? Was he trying to *strangle* you?" His voice cracked as he said that.

"I - I just don't know," I stuttered. He shook his head and turned away from me for a second.

"Listen man, I don't know who the hell you really are, but you can't do that shit." His eyes were full of hurt and were now glossy as he looked at Trevor, all bloodied and bruised.

Trevor was in such critical condition, he was practically unresponsive. Salem carried on. "Why? Do you see what you just did to her? Do you see the bruises on her neck? This is bullshit. Complete utter bullshit," he sputtered.

He grabbed the collar of Trevor's t-shirt and shook him vigorously. "You're sick, man. *Son of a bitch.*" He said those words slowly but sharply. He dropped Trevor back to the floor and tried to keep his composure. I already knew Trevor would probably be dead if I wasn't in the room.

My hearing was finally stabilized again. That was when I heard the sirens. Blaring from outside. I knew this wasn't going to be good.

I had no idea what I was going to say, or how the real truth would be brought to the police. But I had to find a way to show them. After gaining some of my strength back, of course.

Chapter 18:

I could hear banging on the front door. I couldn't open it even if I wanted to, because I was still too weak to stand. Not that I wanted to.

I looked at Salem, and he froze. "Police!" I heard a booming voice yell. Salem was still frozen in fear, and there was no way Trevor could wobble downstairs to the door. More knocking, until eventually I heard the dreaded crash of the door being bashed in.

Salem was about to bolt towards the window in an attempt to escape, but I stopped him. "Don't. You'll make this worse."

Salem stopped and sighed. I guess he too realized it would be better on his behalf to explain the situation to the police rather than run away. He backed away from the closed door of the room we were in and waited with unease.

"Police. We are coming upstairs!" I could hear a few officers storming up the stairs in their heavy gear.

"In here!" I called out desperately. I closed my eyes and prayed as I heard them coming closer and closer. When they finally burst through the door, Salem was the first person they saw.

"Put your hands up! Do not move!" I cried silently as I watched them point a pistol a few inches from Salem's chest.

"Don't shoot!" I begged. The officer pointing the gun kept his focus solely on Salem. "Young man," said the officer, "serious allegations have been made against you. You could be facing both state and federal charges for an alleged kidnapping. Now, you are going to explain to me what is going on here and why two people are critically wounded next to you."

He glanced at Trevor and I on the ground. "And don't make a move. Any sudden movement of any sort will be posed as a threat and could get you shot, you understand?"

Salem remained silent.

"I said, do you understand me?" He hissed. Salem looked him dead in the eye and said with little emotion, "Yes sir."

"Speak. Remember, anything you say or do can and will be used against you in court." I wanted so badly to intervene and tell the cops he was innocent, but I had to remember this wasn't some crazy action movie.

Whatever you do Salem, don't you dare move a muscle and risk getting your head blown off.

Salem tried his best not to fidget or make a wrong move. "Well sir," he projected, "I was on the run. But it was for something I didn't do. I wanted to check in on my friend and had no ill intentions." When he paused and got no reaction from the officer, he continued.

"When I tried the door and found it was unlocked, I headed upstairs to look for Lana and at least get some answers. When I stepped in here after hearing screams, I saw Trevor with his hands pressed on Lana's neck. He was choking her, sir. I had to stop him."

His gaze drifted into space as he waited for a response. "These are serious allegations, Mr. Coleman. Does anyone in this room object to these allegations?"

Trevor, still seemingly fighting for his life, raised his hand. "That kid is a danger to society. I would never try to hurt her like that," he choked.

That was when I decided to come forward. "He's lying. While in this room, I uncovered some serious clues that make it obvious he is a killer. I was supposed to be his next victim, sir."

The lead officer's eyes widened as I said this. "We have a team of people that'll take care of all this." The officer scanned the room and the messy floor.

"The paramedics just pulled in. You, boy. Get on the ground and lay flat." His gun was still loaded and aimed.

Salem, who now looked terrified, carefully lowered himself to the ground until his stomach touched the floor.

"David, get out the handcuffs," said the officer, now staring at one of his partners. The other officer, named David, grabbed a pair of handcuffs from his police uniform and proceeded to cuff Salem.

"What are you doing?" I asked in horror. "You can't arrest him. He didn't do anything wrong!"

The officer shoved his gun back in his holster after Salem was detained. "We are taking Mr. Coleman to the station for questioning. He is to be in police custody until further notice." His eyes said it all. This was serious.

"You're putting him in a jail cell? With - metal bars and stuff?" I gasped.

The officer nodded. "There are two different claims here. There will most likely be a trial involved since the real truth has yet to be discovered."

I don't want to get much into detail. To sum things up, I was later hauled into an ambulance where I was once again without Salem. Just as I had hoped things would go back to normal, Salem was now in handcuffs and I was on a stretcher. But at least I knew that he hadn't been shot, and that he was here, and not halfway across the country.

He might be in a jail cell right now, or in the back of a cop car, but at least he was *alive*.

As for Trevor, he was taken right to the hospital because of his critical injuries. It didn't help the fact that he was old, and more fragile. But did I care? That's what I kept asking myself on the way to the emergency room.

I thought Trevor was a good guy, and he surely was clever. It was a shame he used his smarts to take people's lives away from them. But what was his motive?

I had no idea what was to come next. I heard something about a trial.

It was obvious Trevor wasn't going to accept a plea deal, for why should he? He had so much money. He could afford the best lawyers and defenders.

As for Salem, he was basically broke. Any money he had was gone because of his love for alcohol, cigarettes, and drugs. He was most likely going to settle with a public defender, but that was better than nothing.

I had uncovered so many clues in that room to prove Trevor guilty, but was that going to be enough to throw him in prison? I couldn't describe how powerless I felt as I watched Salem get a gun pointed to his chest and cuffs locked on his wrists. I couldn't help but imagine in ten years from now, would Salem be talking to me through glass in an orange jumpsuit?

It was Trevor who needed to suffer the consequences of his actions, not Salem. But how much power were you entitled to when you were swimming in money? Way too much, unfortunately. Especially if it were a psychological genius swimming in that money.

We had arrived at the hospital, and despite feeling better, I was still required to see a medical professional. I guess they wanted to make sure I hadn't snapped a bone in my neck or something.

I was now in a hospital room shared with another girl who looked to be even younger than I was. There was a curtain dividing us, but when I had caught a glimpse of her, I could see she was on a ventilator.

"Hello, Lana! I'm nurse Pamela, and I'm here to check on you." She flashed me one of those fake smiles that you give children when they're scared of needles. I didn't smile back.

"Let's go ahead and take your temperature. How are you feeling, honey?" she asked as she grabbed a thermometer hanging off the wall.

"I feel fine," I said. "When can I leave?"

Nurse Pamela laughed with her heavy southern accent that practically gave me cavities. I kept my thoughts to myself and waited for an actual response.

"You shouldn't be here for long. We just have to make sure those neck arteries are working alright."

I rolled my eyes. My neck felt fine aside from a few bruises. "Can't you just give me some Advil and send me on my way?" I muttered.

Pamela's smile turned into a look of concern. "You sure don't want to be here, huh. Everything okay?" I didn't even know where to begin.

"I'm going through stuff." Was that the best way to put it? I was strangled by my therapist who's also most likely a serial killer. I thought my best friend was dead until I realized he's being falsely imprisoned instead. I watched him beat the life out of my therapist who diagnosed me with Stockholm Syndrome, and on top of all that, I still didn't have a place to call home. I'd say I'm going through a lot more than just some "stuff".

The upcoming trial I was supposed to attend sounded like a nightmare. I pinched myself to make sure I wasn't dreaming, but after a painful pinch, Nurse Pamela was still towering over me with a thermometer in her hand. This was far from a scary dream.

I stayed overnight at the hospital.

It was pretty scary, considering no one came to visit me in my hospital gown. Salem was in police custody, and I didn't have any other relatives that cared enough to reach out, hence why I was stuck at the orphanage for so long.

Phoebe couldn't visit even if she wanted to because she was in another city and lost contact with me. I was sure my story was going to be on the news at some point, but it wasn't ending anytime soon.

I was finally discharged from the hospital and driven to the police station because I had the answers they were looking for.

As soon as I walked inside, I noticed Detective Lars sipping coffee. "Lana," he said with a grin. "It's great to see you again. If you don't mind, let's head into the back room so we can chat."

I had no idea what that meant, but there was no fighting it at this point. I followed Lars into an office that I assumed was his and sat down.

"I'm sure you're already aware of everything that's going on," he said calmly. "I hate to put so much pressure on you, but you're a witness and we count your claims as credible.

Dr. MacQuoid's house is under investigation. Criminal investigators were able to find and take pictures of several different clues found in that room. Tell me, do any of these clues look familiar to you?"

He clicked through a slideshow of different pieces of evidence. Of course they looked familiar to me. Most of them were in my hands not too long ago.

"Yes, sir. I was the one who found the birthday card laying on the floor. I also uncovered the ID cards in the second picture."

Lars nodded and took notes. "The Identification Cards were all confirmed to be authentic. Any idea why Dr. MacQuoid would have them?"

I shook my head. "The most logical explanation is that he's guilty. He tried to kill me."

Lars cleared his throat. "Now, we can't jump to conclusions yet, can we? Everything you tell me will be thoroughly investigated before we take real action."

I shrugged. "Can you at least let me in on what the deal is with Salem?" I asked. "I'm worried. Like, what is he doing right now? Aside from rotting in a jail cell, of course," I said sarcastically.

Lars chuckled. "Don't worry about Mr. Coleman right now. He hasn't been convicted for anything. A trial will be held in a few weeks to determine his fate. You'll be there to testify for or against him."

Woah. I've never been in court before. "I'm testifying against Trevor," I declared. I could tell Lars was getting slightly impatient.

"Enough about the trial. We have other things to deal with that come first. Like the birthday card. Did you notice the woman who wrote the card to Dr. MacQuoid signed the name 'Debbie'?"

I nodded. "I picked up on that too. They had to have had some sort of relationship with each other, right?"

Lars pulled up another picture on his desktop computer. "It's funny you say that. Not only is the Polaroid picture inside the card a picture of Debbie with Dr. MacQuoid, but our investigators found this document stuffed under a dresser in the room."

I couldn't believe my eyes. In this picture was a crumpled-up divorce paper. But this wasn't any divorce paper - this was a declaration of Debbie Stallard's divorce from Trevor.

Did this mean they were married? That made so much sense.

I guess Lars noticed the shocked expression on my face, because he looked at me and asked, "Have you seen this paper before?"

I shook my head. "I had no idea they were married. When did they divorce?"

"Well, according to the document, they divorced in 2002. That was three years ago."

"Wow. That has to mean something. Trevor has to be a prime suspect in her murder now, right?"

"I can't confirm anything, but I can assure you this won't be swept under the rug. All of the evidence found has been collected and sent to a forensic laboratory."

I took a sigh of relief as I stepped out of Detective Lars's office. I felt better knowing Trevor had so much evidence against him. Surely there was no way he'd win this, right?

I sat and waited in the lobby for Lars. He was the lead detective, and because I could no longer stay with Trevor, Lars offered to let me stay with him until the trial was held.

I'm pretty sure the main reason Lars made such an offer was because this was a big case and he wanted all the details from me; so he could perform his job better. But regardless of his actual intentions, I was grateful.

Although I didn't know him too well, anything was better than going back to the orphanage. I dodged a bullet with that one.

I climbed into Lars's car and shut the door. Lars got into the front seat and started up the engine.

"So Lana," he began, "I'm not sure how long you'll be staying with me, but just know, I don't bite. This is just a temporary arrangement because you don't really have a place to stay." He flashed me a look of pity.

"I won't make you go back to the orphanage, especially because it's important you don't give out any personal details regarding this case. You understand that, right?" He asked as he turned the steering wheel.

"Of course," I said. I've been through this before after Salem was accused of kidnapping me. "Do you know when the trial will be held?"

Lars turned off the radio and pulled into a narrow driveway. "Soon," he said. "Don't you worry about that yet."

Chapter 19:

It was the next morning. My first night at Lars's house had been a success.

Lars and his wife, Porschia, were lovely. They weren't millionaires with a rich mansion like Trevor, but something in the air just felt so comfortable.

I slept like a baby the night before because I was so exhausted. It felt nice waking up in a small, secure room with normal clothes on rather than a hospital gown.

As soon as I stepped out of the room, the first thing I asked Lars was if he had any new updates. "Anything new?" I asked with hope.

He shook his head. "Not yet. I'll be back at the station later today. The evidence is still being processed at the lab, and an official court date hasn't been disclosed yet."

I tried to hide my disappointment. It had only been less than a day. Of course this stuff wouldn't magically settle overnight. "What about Trevor?" I asked. "Where is he?"

Lars grabbed a glass from a cabinet and filled it up with water. "Well, the last time I heard anything about Dr. MacQuoid was last night. He's still in the hospital." He grimaced.

"The kid beat him up pretty badly, you know. Where did he learn to punch like that?"

I thought for a moment. Where had Salem learned how to throw punches and kicks at someone?

"He got into a lot of fights at the orphanage," I said. "And he ran away a lot. I'm not exactly sure of his background. He's a pretty private person - but he's not a criminal."

Lars had a blank expression on his face, and I couldn't read his mind. Did he believe me when I said Salem wasn't a criminal?

I had so many questions, but I had to remember that Lars was still a detective who worked for the police. There had to be some sort of professional barrier between us, even if I was temporarily rooming with him.

I ate a protein bar and drank a cup of coffee to help me get back to my senses. I was feeling pretty drowsy, despite having already finished the cup.

Lars was getting ready to go to work, and given that Porchia worked as a waitress, I had to go to the station with Lars. I didn't mind this, considering every time I stepped into that place I was one step closer to helping close the case that turned my life upside down.

Lars was busy preparing search warrants for other cases, and filing documents that contained private information. I simply kept quiet and occasionally stopped into the lobby to talk to other officers off duty. I was eventually called into his office because he had good news for me.

"I just got off the phone with a judge in the area. Her name is Judge Morris. Things are moving pretty fast, kiddo. Sure this isn't too much for you?"

I laughed. "Just tell me the news already," I said impatiently.

"According to Judge Morris, she wants to get the trial out of the way. We haven't settled an exact date yet, but the trial should begin within the next few weeks or so. Do you think you'd be ready?"

I nodded. I had to make an appearance in court, and I had initially planned to testify against Trevor. This plan wasn't going to change, and the sooner the trial, the fresher the events were in my mind.

Even though my brain wouldn't be forgetting those events anytime soon.

The next day we were in the car driving to the station, which had become pretty normal to me. Lars was driving and I was in the passenger seat, staring out the window. And no, I wasn't looking for Salem this time. I knew exactly where he was.

But even though the radio was on, and Lars was playing his favorite rock music, the car still felt quiet.

He broke the silence by saying, "The trial is approaching. How're you feeling?"

I shrugged. "Mixed emotions."

"How so?"

"Well, I'm really nervous but I'm excited to see Salem again."

He went silent for a minute and I could hear his music still playing as I waited for him to respond.

"I know I'm not your father, and maybe it's not my place to say this, but I don't think you should be hanging around that kid."

I was slightly taken aback by his words. "What?"

"Look, being a dad myself, and a detective, I can tell he's the type of guy you don't want to involve yourself with."

I laughed. "Are you saying I shouldn't be excited to see him?"

He sighed. "Well, I know you don't want to hear this, but it's the truth. Lana, I've seen all his records. And they're not very clean."

"I know they aren't. But I've known him since he was a kid, and he's only like that when he has to be."

"No one's forcing him to drink, or smoke, or go to strip clubs."

I scoffed. "Strip clubs?"

He shook his head. "Have you seen the guy? I mean, I wouldn't put it past him."

"Do you have any faith in him?" I asked in disbelief.

"No."

My eyes went blurry and I decided arguing with my only caregiver right now wasn't worth it. So I dropped the argument.

"I'm sorry Lana, but I want to see what's best for you, and he's just not a good influence."

I swallowed. "So what do you want me to do about it?"

He shrugged. "I can't force you to do anything, but can I just ask you to do one thing for me?"

I stared at him intently as he focused on the road. "Do what?"

"Take my advice."

Chapter 20:

"Are you awake yet?"

It was Lars. A few weeks had passed, and not much had changed. "Of course I'm awake," I muttered. "I couldn't get any sleep."

Lars chuckled and pointed to the clock hanging on the wall. "It's time to get up," he said.

"Do I have to go?" I whined.

He nodded. "I've been to countless trials before. You'll be fine."

I finally stood. I was terrified. Today marked the official date of the trial. The trial that would either prosecute Salem and lock him up for life or put the real psycho behind bars. This surely wasn't a fun game to play, and I didn't want to take my chances. But I had no other choice. I brushed my teeth and put on my nicest clothes while waiting for Lars to get ready.

He slid on his dress shoes and walked out the door. I followed him out to his car. "You're gonna be there with me, right?" I asked hopefully. It was safe to say I had formed a pretty trusted bond with Lars because he had taken me under his wing for the past few weeks. And even though he didn't like Salem, I tried not to let it affect my view of him.

As he began driving, he flashed me a look in the rear view mirror that said it all. He wasn't going with me.

"I wish, kiddo. But I wasn't asked to testify." I tried to mask the disappointment by changing the subject. "What are you doing today?" I tugged at my seatbelt anxiously as I waited for his response.

"I have work today," he said. "I'll be working on other cases and multitasking to get things done. But don't you worry about the trial. They'll tell you what to do."

He sounded confident when he said that, which gave me a little relief. But not enough to look forward to this.

We pulled into the parking lot of the courtroom. I staggered out of the car and followed Lars inside.

The building was huge compared to any building I'd ever seen. Not that I'd seen much in my lifetime anyway, considering I had stepped foot into an arcade for the first time not even two months ago.

"Now, remember. This is a courtroom. Watch what you say. Know your rights and your boundaries. Always ask permission if you want to do something. Good luck," said Lars.

"But what are my rights?" I asked him. "Lars?"

I turned around to see him already in his car about to speed to work, I assume. I collected myself and continued inside with a petrified look on my face.

A clerk greeted me inside, but I wasn't paying attention. The first person I saw was Salem, and instantly I ran over to talk to him.

"Ma'am!" The clerk grabbed my arm and pulled me back towards the entrance. "Please take a seat in the black leather chair to the right of Judge Morris."

His voice was stern, and I was taken aback. I shamefully trudged over to the chair I was asked to sit in, but not before glancing at Salem. My heart shattered as I saw him wearing a loose orange jumpsuit and silver handcuffs.

He looked like a criminal from a documentary or something, being cuffed to the table and all. I sat down and smiled at him, to show him how much I missed him. He smiled back weakly, and that's when I noticed how sunken in his face looked.

Dark circles I had never seen on him before were very much visible. I had to stay confident. It was the only way I could give back his freedom.

A man who I assumed was Salem's public defender sat next to him. Judge Morris sat in her seat that overlooked all of the people in the courtroom.

Trevor was eventually wheeled into the courtroom in a wheelchair. My nerves instantly doubled as soon as we made eye contact.

My eyes darted away from his evil, sinister face that I never wanted to see again. I was anxiously fidgeting with my hands until the doors of the courtroom finally shut and locked in place. Then followed by a long, dreaded silence as Salem's attorney shuffled his papers and documents.

"Good morning, all rise." said Judge Morris.

The tension in the room was hard to break. I wasn't sure what to say, or if I was even allowed to speak. But for the record, I kept my mouth shut.

Judge Morris cleared her throat and glared at all the people facing her in the room, including me.

"As of now, all cellular devices should be silenced. The case presented to us today is now in session. I would like you all to refrain from speaking until further notice. My name is Aimee Morris, and I am a judge here in Greenwood, South Carolina."

She then turned her head to face the jury. "Ladies and gentlemen of the jury, I will have you know this is a criminal case regarding defendant Salem Coleman, the eighteen-year-old boy sitting right before us, and Dr. Trevor MacQuoid, a psychiatrist who was assaulted by Mr. Coleman.

Members of the jury, your duty today will be to determine whether the defendant is guilty or not guilty based solely on the facts and evidence provided in this case. Now, is everybody ready to proceed with opening statements?"

Everyone in the room stood to say, "Yes, your honor." A smile spread across Judge Morris's face. "Well then. Mr. Taylor, care to begin?" She was now staring at a man to her right. "Of course," he said.

"My name is Ralph Taylor, and I am the prosecutor in this criminal case. I will be representing the state of South Carolina today." He inhaled and then exhaled, preparing for his statement.

"Now, imagine this. That man right there in the orange jumpsuit was caught beating up Dr. MacQuoid when police arrived to the scene at his house. Kicking, hitting, punching. Yelling every insult he could think to say out loud.

Now, to put things in simple words for the jury, a few different pieces of evidence you will be presented as we move on include but are not limited to police body camera footage of the assault, and detailed descriptions and pictures of Dr. MacQuoid's gruesome injuries filed by doctors and nurses at a local hospital. Potential charges the defendant could face if proven guilty would be Aggravated Battery, and First Degree Kidnapping. But that's a separate charge."

He took a seat and shuffled the papers he had in his hands. "You may carry on, Judge Morris. I've said all I needed to." He motioned for her to continue with instruction.

Judge Morris nodded and cleared her throat. "Thank you, Mr. Taylor. Now for you, sir. Speak loud and clearly please."

The man sitting next to Salem in a collared shirt stood up from his chair.

"Thank you, your honor. I am Kevin Smith, and I am here today to represent Salem Coleman. Something very important you have to note before I proceed is that Salem Coleman assaulted Dr. MacQuoid because his friend, Lana Garcia, was in danger. Salem walked into a small, suspicious room just in the nick of time to find Lana Garcia being strangled to the point where she couldn't breathe. Her face was practically going blue, and after Salem had discovered what was going on, he jumped in to save her.

So yes, he was throwing kicks and punches at Dr. MacQuoid. And sure, his injuries were fatal because of this. But if Salem hadn't jumped in to fight off Dr. MacQuoid when he did, that girl right there probably wouldn't be standing here with us today."

I felt all eyes on me, and I was uncomfortable. But there was no denying this guy was good for a public defender.

I could see Salem smirk as his defender said his piece. Everything Mr. Smith had said was accurate. After all, I was the one being strangled. Which led me to ponder - if Salem hadn't walked in when he did, would I still be here today to witness this trial?

Mr. Smith went on to elaborate more on the pieces of evidence to be used in Salem's favor. He didn't give many details, but I hoped he had enough evidence. After all was said and done, Judge Morris cleared her throat and moved on.

"Thank you, gentlemen. Prosecution, are you ready to proceed to a Direct Examination?"

Mr. Taylor stood from his seat and said, "Why of course, your honor." Then Judge Morris turned over to Salem and his attorney. "Defense, are you ready to proceed?"

Mr. Smith stood to face her and said with confidence, "Yes, your honor."

The first piece of evidence was brought out for the jury to see.

The prosecutor, Mr. Taylor, presented several documents from the hospital Trevor was treated in.

"Ladies and gentlemen of the jury," said Mr. Taylor. "I want you to take a look at these."

He held up the packet of papers that disclosed the exact information needed to prove just how serious Trevor's injuries were. I glanced over at Salem to see him tense up just a little.

I wondered what was running through his mind at that point. How was he not freaking out right now? I know I would be. But this was Salem we were talking about. We weren't exactly the same.

"In these documents provided by the local emergency room here in Greenwood, it's not exactly hard to see that Dr. MacQuoid will not be healing anytime soon. In fact, the defendant caused some serious damage, knocking out two back teeth, fracturing ribs, and even puncturing a lung."

The jury gasped. To be quite honest, I felt like gasping too. Puncturing a lung? How could a fist even do that? Salem looked unfazed, but only because he didn't seem to regret what he did. He was trying to protect me, and he surely succeeded.

"Now, ladies and gentlemen - if you think that's bad, wait till you see this." My stomach churned anxiously as I watched him pull out a set of brass knuckles concealed in a plastic bag.

"I call Dr. MacQuoid to the stands," said Mr. Taylor. He was wheeled to the front of the room.

"Dr. MacQuoid. Do you mind telling the jury what you know about these?" He held a tight grasp onto the knuckles and shook them vigorously.

I felt like throwing up. Salem had beaten Trevor - with brass knuckles? No wonder his lung had been punctured.

I tried replaying the events that took place on the day I was almost strangled. I was too busy trying not to faint to even look at Salem's knuckles while he beat Trevor relentlessly. It wasn't exactly a sight I wanted to see. And worst of all, why would he leave the brass knuckles at the scene? I buried my face into my hands as Trevor started speaking.

"Salem Coleman started throwing punches at me with those knuckles on. I remember them hitting and spiking my chest as I gasped for air. After the police had arrived to arrest him, I guess the knuckles slipped off his right hand. That, or he didn't want the police to see them on him."

Mr. Taylor nodded. "Anything else you know about these brass knuckles that you'd like to tell us, Dr. MacQuoid?"

Trevor shook his head. "I don't know much about them. All I know is that those knuckles are part of the reason as to why I'm in a wheelchair." He was then wheeled back to his original seat, and that was when I finally took my hands off my eyes.

"Now, the last significant piece of evidence I would like to present to the jury is the police body cam footage of Mr. Coleman assaulting Dr. MacQuoid. This is physical evidence that shows exactly what the police officer saw as he stepped into the room. This is authentic evidence that Judge Morris has already approved. Judge Morris, may I roll the footage?"

Judge Morris nodded and the clip was rolled for the jury and everyone else in the room to see.

I was starting to feel sick to my stomach as I watched the clip. It was a pretty brutal attack, that was for sure. But something I hadn't noticed before that I noticed now was the brass knuckles.

Where Salem had gotten them from, I had no idea. I didn't even want to think about the ties he had with people I'd never met before.

Salem's face remained neutral as he watched the footage of himself. He stayed calm and collected throughout the whole proceeding of the video playing, and I wasn't sure whether that was a good or bad thing. It didn't matter though, because now the jury was exchanging worried glances with each other. This wasn't a good sign.

Now, it was the defense's turn to present his evidence.

Mr. Taylor had finally finished presenting his dramatic pieces, and with footage like that, it was hard to say Salem was innocent. But before Mr. Smith presented his evidence, he had a chance to cross-examine Trevor.

"Defense, you may cross-examine Dr. MacQuoid." Mr. Smith stood up from his seat and walked up the podium.

"Dr. MacQuoid. How do you know the brass knuckles belonged to Mr. Coleman? What if, perhaps, you planted them there?"

Trevor grunted. "Well, I know they were Mr. Coleman's because I don't own a pair of brass knuckles. He assaulted me with them in hand. It was very clear in the video." He lifted up part of his shirt to show the bandaged wounds allegedly caused by the brass knuckles.

There was lots of bruising on his stomach surrounding the bandages. "And, if you need actual proof, the brass knuckles were sent into a forensic lab as a piece of authenticated evidence for fingerprints."

"And do you know if they found any fingerprints on the brass knuckles?" Asked Mr. Smith.

"Of course they did. And they belonged to Mr. Coleman." The jury's eyes all widened with this fact. And mine did too.

This wasn't looking good for Salem. *Please*, I thought to myself. *Kevin Smith, prove him otherwise.*

"Any more questions?" Asked Judge Morris.

"No further questions, Your Honor."

Chapter 21:

I tried not to make my disappointment obvious. My gritted teeth fell into a pout as I watched Mr. Smith step away from the podium, defeated.

Could you blame him though? There wasn't really any more questions to ask that could disprove Trevor's statements. If the evidence was there, it was there. You couldn't erase it.

Aside from that setback, I tried not to let it bother me. The trial was just beginning.

Mr. Smith began to present his evidence that would help prove his case of self-defense. I bad no idea what evidence was to be provided, but I was going to wait and see.

"Ladies and gentlemen of the jury," Mr. Smith said confidently. "I would like to show you something extremely important to this case. Something that's not being stressed enough. The horrible markings left on Lana Garcia's neck.

Perhaps I should elaborate a little more. Lana, do you mind stepping up here to show the jury your wounds?"

I nodded hesitantly and walked up to the podium. He smiled and motioned for me to face the jury.

"Ladies and gentlemen, do you notice something here? The very obvious markings on her neck?"

He pointed to the bruises and the puffiness still visible where Trevor had put his hands. "There's a bruise," he said while pointing to one of the many. "And look at that one. Do you see the red marks? The hand marks have since faded and the swelling has gone down after Lana's been treated at the hospital, but allow me to show you pictures taken by the hospital the day of the crime. May I?"

He turned to Judge Morris and made sure he had permission to present the pictures. Judge Morris nodded, and I stood there with a nervous smile as I watched the expressions on the jury's faces.

I had to admit, even I was shocked at the pictures. I guess I hadn't really looked at the damage done on my neck that day. It's not like I wanted to be reminded of what he had done to me, or tried to do. He tried to *kill me*.

"Take a close look. There are very obvious outlines of hands on her neck. But that's not even the shocking part. Dr. MacQuoid, the man who's trying to play the victim here, is the one who inflicted these wounds. The one who deliberately placed his hands on that girl's neck because he wanted to kill her. He wanted her to die that day, and the reason she's still alive and not in a casket right now is because of my loyal client."

Now, he was pointing to Salem. The jury looked amplified. His little speech had struck me differently, and I guess he had that same effect on the now shocked jury.

Trevor was starting to get a little anxious in his seat, and the dirty looks he was now receiving subtly gave me peace of mind. Even Trevor's attorney, who had been paid a lot to be here, was starting to look a little nervous too.

"Judge Morris, that really is the only evidence I need to prove my point. This young lady is walking, breathing proof of why my client should not be prosecuted for doing what he did. You may proceed, Your Honor."

His confidence was radiant, and I loved that. He sounded so much more professional with confidence, and anything that could help prove Salem's innocence was a big deal. I too tried to keep a calm, yet emotional demeanor that I will admit was practiced.

Now, it was time to move on to the Prosecution's Direct Examination of his second witness.

His second witness called to the stands was the police officer who provided the footage of Salem's assault.

The officer's encounter was brief and simple. He stuttered quite a bit after being questioned, and he didn't have much information to give. But after his examination was done, Mr. Smith cross examined the officer to try and unravel his storyline.

It didn't help much. The officer only provided so much information to pull apart. So after that was done, it was time to move on. Mr. Smith was given permission by Judge Morris to bring in his first witness.

By this point my attentiveness was starting to dull. I couldn't recall every little detail, but my heart jumped as soon I heard him say, "I call Lana Garcia to the stands."

I gave him a look that said, *me?* As if I wasn't the only Lana in the room. But after he nodded and flashed me a smile, I had no choice but to join him at the front of the room again.

I looked at Salem who was smiling at me, as if to say, *you got this.* I blushed and tried to keep my focus on what really mattered here. Getting him out of that gross neon jumpsuit and back into my life where I felt he belonged.

"Lana, do you mind if I ask you some questions?" asked Mr. Smith.

I wanted to say no and run out of the room. But this was an active trial. I exhaled and then breathed, "Go right ahead." Damn. Why was my voice so shaky?

"Lana, what do you recall happened on the day of the crime?"

I tapped my foot anxiously as I formed a response in my head. Finally, I opened my mouth, and poured out my side of the story. The truth that needed to be heard and echoed a hundred times.

"The day I got strangled. I won't sugarcoat it. Dr. MacQuoid, as you all refer to him as - I call him Trevor - or at least, I did before I realized he wasn't just my guardian. He was trying to become my murderer."

I smiled before the cracks in my voice became too prominent. "I found this weird room in his house. Found some weird stuff. Next thing you know, his hands were on my neck. That's why I was sent to the hospital while I witnessed my best friend, Salem, being held at gunpoint for getting handsy with my attacker, Trevor MacQuoid." Mr. Smith nodded as he waited for me to continue.

"To sum it up," I continued, "I was strangled that day, and almost died. Trevor won't admit it, but that's exactly what happened. Salem can vouch for me on that one. If he wasn't in cuffs right now, that is. Sitting in jail for beating the man who tried to kill me." I smiled sarcastically.

Before I got too mouthy, I stopped talking and let Mr. Smith take over.

"Thank you, Lana. Now, next question - what was running through your head during the whole event?"

I blinked. "What was running through my head? A lot of emotions. Anger, because I don't think anyone would be happy about being strangled. Sadness, because my therapist and legal guardian who I almost considered a dad tried strangling me. Confusion, because why the hell would I expect to be strangled by the man who was the only person I could depend on? But, most importantly, relief, because after all that, Salem stopped Trevor from strangling me to death." I stared down at my feet because in all honesty, I was spitting out more than I had meant to, and I didn't want to see the expressions of anyone in the room after my harsh exchange.

Mr. Smith cleared his throat and tried to remain professional. "Uh, yes. Thank you Lana. I have one last question for you. A personal question. Who do you think deserves to be in prison after the trial is over?"

"Objection, your Honor. He can't ask that."

I looked up in surprise to see Mr. Taylor, now standing and frowning at Mr. Smith.

Mr. Smith looked to Judge Morris worriedly, wondering if he had made a rookie mistake. Judge Morris pushed the glasses she was wearing up the bridge of her nose and then declared, "Overruled. Mr. Taylor, have a seat and let the girl give her honest testimony."

Mr. Taylor scowled but proceeded to take a seat.

Mr. Smith grinned and finally the room was silent again. Waiting for me to give my honest response. "Well, Mr. Smith, this one is obvious. If anyone in this room is to be sent to prison today, it most certainly won't be Salem if I can help it.

Dr. MacQuoid tried to strangle me. Why he did it, I wouldn't know. But he is the real guilty one here. Salem saved me from him. So to answer your question loud and clear, I am confident that Dr. MacQuoid should be the one sent to prison after all is straightened out. And I hope he never gets out. Not until the day I die."

I took a step back from the podium and tried to stop my lips from quivering with nerves. Did I really just say all that out loud? Without stuttering? Maybe I wasn't all that bad at giving testimonies.

"Thank you, Lana. I have heard all I needed to hear. No further questions, Your Honor."

Judge Morris fixed her posture and clasped her hands together. "Prosecution, you are up for cross-examining Lana Garcia."

Oh god. I was intimidated by Mr. Taylor, to say the least. He had so much experience. Money. Everything the Defense didn't have.

I was worried I would say something to bring us right back to square one. To completely disprove everything I had just raved to the whole courtroom. But I knew myself better than anyone else, and in this moment, I knew I would control my words. For Salem.

I could do this. I could run through a couple stupid questions. Trevor wasn't going to get away with ruining my life and leaving me without my best friend, no matter how much money and power he had.

No murderer deserved to be in any formal position of power. Especially one dealing with the mentally ill. The more vulnerable of the human race that looked to him for guidance, the same way I did when he first diagnosed me with Stockholm Syndrome.

Mr. Taylor cleared his throat and then our eyes met for the first time that day. He had piercing brown eyes that I couldn't stare at for much longer. The coldness he radiated. It made me uncomfortable. But then he spoke. *To me.*

"Lana, I heard you say previously that Salem Coleman didn't deserve to be in prison. With the damage he did, are you sure about that? Or are you biased because he's your friend?"

"Biased? Me? Why the hell would I be -" I stopped myself. I was bad at this. I forgot for a minute I was in a courtroom, being challenged by a lawyer who had been to law school for god knows how long earning actual degrees for these trials. I had to keep my emotion out of this part.

"Sorry. Let me rephrase that. I don't need to be biased to know why your client deserves jail time. He tried to strangle me. *Kill* me. Salem came at the right time and literally saved my life. Why would I let him be prosecuted for that, sir?"

"Okay, Lana. Let me ask you this. Why would someone living a good life with such a stable job risk everything he has going for him by trying to strangle an orphan?"

My mouth fell. I didn't know what to say. I stood there, on the podium, looking like a total dummy. How did he know? Was it obvious I was an orphan? And why did he feel the need to use that against me? Was that even allowed?

My eyes darted to Salem naturally and I could tell he too was taken aback. He sighed and as much as he probably wanted to defend me, he sat there in that chair, powerless and of no authority.

I tried to swallow my senses whole and answer his question. The room was silent. More silent than I was comfortable with. But then I did something kind of stupid.

"Why don't you ask your client that, since clearly he's the only one who would know the answer to your derogatory question?" I spat. "Seriously. Is this how you win all your cases? By belittling people in front of the whole courtroom? This can't be allowed. You can't just expect me to answer a question like that. I mean, *seriously*?" I raged.

"Enough, Lana." It was Judge Morris. "This is court. Do you need a minute? Please step out of the room, and come back in when you are ready to proceed."

My cheeks went hot. I looked around. All eyes were on me, and that's when I realized I just humiliated myself in front of everyone by accident.

Salem. He saw that too, didn't he? *Shit.*

I trudged to the heavy doors and was about to step out. But before I opened them, I looked at Salem and the disappointment on his face is probably what hurt me the most.

I made Salem's defender look bad. I put Salem's life in jeopardy. His future is on the line here, and everything I say and do from this point forward could either save it and his reputation or completely shatter both. The only way I could fix this now was by coming back into the courtroom with a fake smile and a thick, heavy filter.

Chapter 22:

I pushed open the bulky doors to the courtroom and looked around. Everyone had remained in the position I'd left them in.

I swallowed and marched my way back to the podium I was standing at when I had my little outburst. The sound of my flats hitting the floor was practically echoing in the room with how silent everyone was.

"I'd like to apologize," I murmured. "I am ready to continue my questioning, Your Honor." Judge Morris, with no emotion, turned to Mr. Taylor and asked, "Mr. Taylor, are you ready to pick up where we left off?"

Mr. Taylor, who clearly did not take a liking to me, especially after the stunt I just pulled, nodded. "Yes Your Honor." After a minute of silence, he asked me another question. A new one, I noticed.

"Lana, I know you were seeing my client for medical help regarding mental issues. He is a psychiatrist, after all. One of the most reliable in town. Could these medical issues alter what you really think happened on the day of the crime?"

I rolled my eyes. If only he knew I didn't actually have any "mental issues". But I was going to develop some if I saw Salem get arrested today.

"No sir. I don't actually have any mental issues. And even if I did, I don't necessarily think that would mess with what I saw. I know what

I saw, and I told you exactly what I saw." I made sure to make that very clear for everyone in the room.

"Ah, but that's where you're wrong. You were recently diagnosed with Stockholm Syndrome by my client. One of the smartest psychiatrists here in South Carolina. I've seen your files. Could this be why you're defending Salem? I see a correlation there."

This was Trevor's plan all along. He knew exactly what he was doing. Smart man, but pure evil.

My eyes skidded over to where he was sitting. He smirked, and I gritted my teeth. A mental genius who was also a suspected serial killer. How was I supposed to prove this guy wrong, and in front of so many people?

"I don't have Stockholm Syndrome, sir. Dr. MacQuoid did that on purpose. To try and disprove my statements. But no, that wouldn't be why I'm defending Salem. I'm defending him because he saved my life."

I could tell Mr. Taylor was starting to run out of ideas. He couldn't cough up any more pathetic questions to try and throw me off guard.

"No further questions, Your Honor." And just like that, I was finally allowed to flee back to the comfort of my seat, and not in front of scary adults wearing nice suits and dress shoes.

My questioning was done. For now at least. I let that sink in. Relief washed over me, and I smiled at Salem. He weakly smiled back.

That was all I needed to know I was saying the right things while facing such a scary position. But now what? I looked over at Judge Morris, who was staring at everyone coldly.

"Prosecution. Do you have any more witnesses or pieces of evidence you would like to present to us today?" Mr. Taylor muttered, "No, Your Honor." And thank god for that.

"Defense, do you have any more pieces of evidence or witnesses to bring to the stands today?" Mr. Smith noticeably was looking stressed. "Uh, yes Your Honor. He's just - running late. He should be here any minute now."

Mr. Smith looked around the room, as if to spot something, or someone. "Is there someone you are expecting?" Asked Judge Morris.

"Yes Your Honor," said Mr. Smith. "I'm sorry. He should've been here by now." Judge Morris tried not to look too annoyed when she said, "We can't sit here and wait for a witness if they aren't going to show."

Who was he expecting? I don't remember this being part of the plan.

Was there really anyone else at this point that could testify against Trevor? It wasn't like I knew anybody outside of the orphanage back in North Augusta. And as for Mr. Smith, I didn't know much about the guy. He was assigned to this case, and Salem didn't pay him anything to be here. He had no money to give. What was the hold up?

Everyone was getting ancy in their seats, but Judge Morris had no time to fool around. "Well, perhaps we should move on to the next step. Prosecution, are you ready to -"

There was a knock at the door. A loud one. Judge Morris was cut off and visibly agitated. A clerk opened the heavy doors and inside stepped the last person I would expect to be here.

Mr. Smith's eyes lit up as he saw the man who walked in, and Trevor's challenging eyes were now looking panicked, which only complimented his mouth now agape with shock. I too was freaking out. The man walking inside the courtroom right now was the one and only mysterious blonde guy with the canary tattoo.

Who was this guy, and why were we crossing paths again? Or, more importantly, might I wonder, why was he a part of Salem's trial?

Wearing a ruffled unbuttoned polo and casual jeans was *the* canary guy. His blonde hair looked a mess and he was clearly not prepared to be here.

"So sorry I'm late," he declared as he took a seat. I lost track of time."

Mr. Smith proudly stood and claimed his place at the front of the courtroom again. "I would like to call my last and final witness to the stands."

Everyone watched as the mysterious canary guy sauntered to the podium. This guy was supposed to testify for Salem? Who *was* he?

Judge Morris, who was still not overly thrilled of the late subject, shook her head. "Would you mind telling us your name before you begin your questioning, sir?"

"My name?" The canary guy asked. "Oh. Right. You guys need to know that stuff. I can tell you someone who knows exactly who I am. He's actually sitting right over there in the wheelchair." He pointed to Trevor, who was still frozen in shock, now staring at the canary guy.

"But for the rest of you who probably have no idea who I am, my name is Hudson MacQuoid."

Chapter 23:

Oh my god. Now I was the one gawking at the canary guy. I couldn't even call him that anymore.

He had a name, and I knew that name. It didn't take long to connect the dots. MacQuoid? That wasn't exactly a common last name. *Hudson*.

Flashbacks from the very day I met Trevor were all coming back. The day he told me about his dead son. *This was my son, Hudson's room. That was his name.* That's exactly what he told me. But wait a minute - did that mean Trevor didn't actually have a dead son? That his "dead" son was actually right here in front of us all along? That I had been simultaneously running into Trevor MacQuoid's son all these months, before I even met Trevor himself, and had somehow given him the name "canary guy" in my head?

It was him. Reality was starting to sink in, and at an alarming rate. This mysterious guy with a yellow canary tattoo on his neck was ironically the son of Trevor, who I thought was dead up until now. Not only that, but this man was also being brought into Salem's trial as a witness for the defense and I still couldn't figure out why, or what relevance he had.

All my questions were soon to be answered as I heard Judge Morris finally say, "Defense, you may now examine your last witness."

"Thank you for your presence, Hudson. I was worried you wouldn't show. You are a very important element in proving my client's case here. You know a lot about Dr. MacQuoid, I'm sure. Would you mind telling us who you are?" asked Mr. Smith.

"Sure thing. I'm Hudson, the son of Trevor MacQuoid. A psychiatrist who I'm sure you all have heard of by now if you're sitting in this room."

Mr. Smith nodded in amazement. "Thank you. Now, assuming that you're already familiar with the case brought up here today in the courtroom, do you or do you not believe Mr. Coleman's case of defense?"

"I do. Dr. MacQuoid might be my dad, but there's so much I know about him that the media doesn't. If you told me with no evidence that he placed his hands on that girl, I wouldn't have a doubt. And given that you do have the evidence to prove this, that just gives me more of a reason to believe you."

"And why are you so confident that your dad could do something like this?" Mr. Smith queried.

"Well, after what he did to my mom . . ." He trailed off, now staring spitefully at his father.

"Dad, I didn't want anything to happen to you. So I kept this burden a secret for so long. But now that I've heard you've done it again - and again - well, it's time for me to say something."

Trevor tensed up in his wheelchair with gritted teeth. "What are you on about, boy? Quit the bluff."

Everyone looked around, now stunned, and at a loss of what to expect. So many things were all happening at once.

Judge Morris cleared her throat and tapped her gavel lightly on the counter. "Dr. MacQuoid, you are of no authority to speak right now. Let Hudson give his honest testimony."

Hudson continued as everyone remained quiet. "There's no putting it lightly. My dad has helped so many people struggling with their battles. And I know what I'm about to say might be hard to believe. But it's all true. My dad . . . he killed my mom."

Everyone was in shock. Several gasps could be heard. My mouth fell. But that's not all he had to say. "He didn't just kill my mom. He killed two other women. The two women in the paper who were recently murdered also died in the hands of my father."

Trevor was practically fuming at this point. He cleared his throat loud enough to cut off his son. "Oh, come on now. You all are just gonna believe what this stupid teenager says?"

Hudson looked visibly hurt. "I'm not a teenager anymore, dad. It's been years. I'm twenty-one."

"I don't care how old you are, boy. You have no proof to support your absurd claims. You just want to see your successful old man crumble, don't you?" Trevor declared.

"Actually, I do have proof. I'll let Mr. Smith take over for that."

"One more question before you step away from the podium," said Mr. Smith. "What was the name of your mother, Hudson?"

Hudson, who still had his eyes on Dr. MacQuoid, said, "Deborah Stallard. He called her Debbie."

I knew that name. *Debbie Stallard.* She was one of the three victims in the paper. And Trevor allegedly murdered her. Why?

Mr. Smith smiled wide and thanked Hudson for his testimony.
G
"Now, as far as the proof for Hudson's accusations against Dr. MacQuoid, the authorities were able to uncover a document that is vital to the case. May I present this to the jury, Your Honor?" He asked.

Judge Morris agreed, and we all watched as Mr. Smith pulled out a paper wrapped in plastic.

"This, ladies and gentlemen, is an authentic divorce paper between Trevor MacQuoid and his then wife, Deborah Stallard. Debbie, the same woman who was murdered by someone just recently. Wouldn't that make Dr. MacQuoid a very obvious suspect in Deborah's sudden murder?"

As Mr. Smith held it proudly for the whole courtroom to fix their eyes on, I waited for the next step he was going to take.

"Alright everyone," he said, "let's not get too distracted by that paper. After all, it's not the only piece of evidence that proves Dr. MacQuoid was once married to murder victim Deborah Stallard. Amongst the chaos of Dr. MacQuoid's secret room, this birthday card addressed to Dr. MacQuoid was found on the floor. And, to no surprise, it was from his ex-lover Debbie."

He then held up the birthday card I had discovered and dropped in Trevor's secret room.

I had found that card. I felt like some sort of admired detective. I guess I hadn't really realized just how much of a role I played in this case, that was now turning into a murder trial. But wait a minute. The Polaroid. It was in the card. Where was it? That would be the cherry on top.

And, almost like it was on cue, Mr. Smith pulled the musty Polaroid out of the card and showed it to the Jury.

"This is an authentic Polaroid taken back when Dr. MacQuoid and Debbie Stallard were husband and wife. All of this is concrete evidence that the two were very close to each other. Clearly, Dr. MacQuoid could easily be the one behind Debbie's murder. Which would mean he'd be automatically linked to the two other murders here in Greenwood, and the attempted murder of Lana Garcia. I rest my case."

"Oh, please," said Mr. Taylor. "Even if your accusations are true, how would that make my client automatically responsible for his ex-wife's murder?" v78tfq9

"I thought you'd never ask," Mr. Smith laughed. "First of all, they're divorced. Clearly the two divorced for a reason. A happy couple wouldn't divorce just because. Second of all, you may notice on the divorce document that Deborah did not have Dr. MacQuoid's last name, even while they were married. According to Hudson, Debbie refused to change her last name, despite Dr. MacQuoid's many attempts to get her to do so. Because of Dr. MacQuoid's high status, this was a big deal to him. An argument later aroused, and their marriage never fully recovered after that hiccup."

Mr. Taylor cleared his throat as if to subtly announce he had nothing else to say. The courtroom was silent for a moment, but Judge Morris quickly fixed the tension by formally allowing Mr. Taylor to cross examine Hudson.

"Well, Hudson. I see you've made a lot of accusations that quite frankly have nothing to do with the case we've been presented with." Mr. Taylor grinned sarcastically and stuffed his hands into his fancy pant pockets.

"Actually, sir, I think they very much correlate with the case here against the young man who helped Lana Garcia. He pummeled my dad, righteously so, after he tried to add her name to his killing streak. I think I can safely say I know my father better than anyone else in this room. I know his real intentions, and they're evil."

"Were you at the scene of the crime, where Dr. MacQuoid was brutally assaulted by Mr. Coleman?" Asked Mr. Taylor.

"No, I was not."

"Then why are you here? Why are you here to testify against my client, who is bandaged and in a wheelchair?"

"Because your client is my dad, and my dad is a sick person who murders women after the fallout between him and my mom, and the man collects their IDs as some sort of deranged trophy," Hudson affirmed. "There. The secret's out, dad. You took my mom away. And now you need to pay the price. So you can't hurt families anymore. Innocent people. Lana, I'm sorry." He buried his face in his hands on the podium as he tried to contain himself.

Mr. Taylor was about to press him again, but Judge Morris interrupted. "Give him a minute, Mr. Taylor."

Hudson finally stood up straight and managed to harness his emotions. "Mr. Smith, I'll let you continue."

Mr. Smith nodded. "Thank you, Hudson. Ladies and gentlemen, as heard directly from Dr. MacQuoid's son himself, the man collects each victim's ID as some sort of reward after murdering them. Don't believe me? These were all confiscated right from the room Lana was almost strangled in."

And just as I had hoped, Mr. Smith held up the wallet I had stumbled upon moments before those hands were on my neck.

Chapter 24:

So where was I again? Right. The wallet.

Mr. Smith eagerly tore open the wallet to reveal it's contents. An ID card fell to the floor and he picked it up as fast as it dropped.

"There it is. Felicia White. The woman who was just murdered. Why would Dr. MacQuoid have Felicia White's ID card if he had nothing to do with her murder?" He set the card on a table in front of him and pulled out the next one.

"Serenity Hall. Another recent murder victim."

He then pulled out the third. "Deborah Stallard. Ex-wife. Another murder victim, coincidentally a woman, who was once married to Dr. MacQuoid. And now she's dead and all that's left of her is this flimsy card. In Dr. MacQuoid's house."

Everyone studied the card he was holding up with wide eyes. But the most important one, that would show everybody why these crimes were all linked to each other, was my card.

Mr. Smith pulled the last card out of the not-so dainty wallet and flipped it towards the jury.

"Can someone from the Jury please tell me what name is printed on this card?" He asked the crowd on the sidelines.

Someone finally read out, "Lana Garcia." I swallowed my nerves and tried not to look so dumbfounded when I heard my name. It was still weird hearing people I barely knew use it so much.

"That's not mine!" Dr. MacQuoid sprang up angrily and pointed at the wallet still in Mr. Smith's hands. "I don't know where you found that ugly thing, but I've never seen it or those cards before."

The jury gasped. I gasped. Judge Morris blinked a couple times in shock. We all witnessed the same thing. I could've sworn I heard Salem laugh. Dr. MacQuoid had stood - in a *wheelchair*.

After realizing the mistake he had made, he fell back into the wheelchair. He yelped in pain and grasped his chest as if that would make it believable. But to my dismay, no one bought it.

"You fake!" Mr. Smith yelled. Someone from the jury scoffed loud enough for Dr. MacQuoid to hear. "You're not really injured enough to be in a damn wheelchair," Mr. Smith continued. Dr. MacQuoid started to look panicked.

"Now, everyone, my client just got ancy and had to address the lies being spread about him. He got this wheelchair from the hospital," Mr. Taylor corrected.

For the first time today, I heard Salem clearly speak. "You're pathetic," he uttered. "Someone lock this guy up already!"

The jury seemed to like this idea because suddenly there was a lot of noise coming from that side of the room. Things like, "Yeah!" or, "Fake!" could be heard amongst the uncontrolled arousal.

Judge Morris tapped her gavel against her desk, this time loud enough to shut everyone up. "Quiet in my court!" She demanded. "We have not reached the end of this hearing. Everyone is to refrain from the unnecessary comments. I'd like to hear what the Defense has to say."

"If you still don't believe Dr. MacQuoid could hurt Lana Garcia, there was a motive. A theory that makes perfect sense. This wallet? Ms. Garcia found the wallet in that room and opened it." Mr. Smith opened the wallet.

"And then she looked through the cards," he said while slowly pulling out the ID cards one by one. He let the first three drop to the floor.

"Until she saw her own card, with her face on it." He held up my ID card.

"And then, Dr. MacQuoid came into the room, saw Lana discovering a secret that could ruin his life, his career - and he *grabbed* her. Strangled her - to silence her." He vigorously shook his hands now cupped in front of him.

"And then," he breathed, "In comes my client who saved his best friend from Dr. MacQuoid. He beats him out of anger." He proceeds to punch the air a couple times while eyeing Dr. MacQuoid.

"He came to the right place at the right time. See how much sense this makes? Jury, I ask you to seriously consider this theory. My client is no kidnapper; he is not a stupid teenager who deserves to be imprisoned. Salem Coleman saved Lana Garcia from her life at the orphanage and he upheld his promise of protecting her."

And that was his closing statement. The theory, the evidence, the passion - it was all so authentic.

Salem had the upper hand now. But Dr. MacQuoid, despite slipping up more than once, was still competition. And I couldn't get cocky just yet.

As Mr. Smith proudly went to take his seat, he thought for a second and jumped up. "The gift!" He exclaimed. "Uh, Judge Morris, there is one more piece of evidence I need to present. It will seal my whole case. I'm so sorry I didn't present it sooner."

Judge Morris hesitated but then rolled her eyes and muttered, "Very well, Mr. Smith. Proceed with your final piece of evidence."

Mr. Smith looked like he had just won the lottery as he shuffled in a briefcase. How much evidence did this guy have? I mean, I wasn't complaining. I just wish he had organized it all better. But it was his first case, and I had to give it to him; he was still pretty amazing.

Mr. Smith finally found the little box I hadn't seen in months. Something I had completely forgotten about. The pink sparkly box. And the card I had handwritten for him.

Salem never opened that gift, and this had just dawned on me now. And maybe that was for the best, because now I remembered exactly why this gift was such a valuable element to Mr. Smith's case.

"Ladies and gentlemen of the Jury, may I have your attention one last time? I would like to present something you have to see before making your decision."

Mr. Smith held up the delicate box for everyone to see before carefully untying the ribbon that held it together. He then pulled off the top of the box, and I mentally prepared myself for what he was about to reveal.

"This here is a gift Lana Garcia gave to Salem the day he aged out of the orphanage. It was a birthday gift. However, my client never had the chance to open that gift, and we were lucky enough to find it in his backpack untouched the day it was confiscated for evidence."

He started by showing what was inside the box. It was a silver heart locket, one that I'd saved up for, and inside the heavy locket stored a little picture of the two of us. Only, we were so young and it was a picture freshly taken the first week I had arrived at my new environment.

It felt like forever ago when that picture was taken, but something significant about the picture was the fact that we looked inseparable here; like we didn't even need anyone but each other's company.

That was before Salem started smoking and downing booze, but his personality never changed from the little Salem I met years ago.

I could tell by the way Salem's eyes glossed and his overwhelmed expression that this was his first time seeing the locket and its contents. It was a shame he discovered the gift in a trial that could easily put him away for life, but the fact that his reaction was still pure made the money worth it.

But I guess what mattered more right now was the jury's expressions. Some lady cooed and another guy smiled when he saw the picture up close in Mr. Smith's hands.

"If you still have the impression my client kidnapped Lana Garcia, maybe this will give you a better perspective. The two were always around each other even when they were kids. However, that's not all. Along with the locket and this picture was a card, handwritten by Lana a week prior to Salem's dismissal. Before Salem could even think about 'kidnapping' his best friend. Allow me to read it to you."

Oh god. Salem, you're either about to distance yourself from me forever or find my little letter adorable. Maybe both. Maybe neither.

"This is what her note reads." He held the crinkled paper in one hand and the torn pink envelope in the other.

Dear Salem,
knowing you won't be nearly as close to me after you're gone has totally been painful to think about. Whatever you choose to do from here . . . well, I hope it's a good choice. When I won't be there to keep you out of trouble, God only knows what you'll get into. But when you save up for a phone call me. If you go broke - write me a letter like this one. Did you know they have plenty of paper here? I would write to you all the time, but you probably won't have an actual address. So where would I send it to? Okay, enough stalling. I think over the past few years, I've realized something. I kinda like you. Like, not just as a stupid brother or something, but you're more

than family to me. If you feel the same, great. We can plan out our futures together or something. But if not, I guess that's cool too. I still wish you nothing but the best. Thank you for making me feel a little less dejected after I lost my grandma. Thank you for making me feel like I can rely on someone. And thank you for always feeling the need to check up on me; to make me feel loved. Like I belong somewhere. Goodbye Salem. I hope you think about me too.
Love, Lana

Yeah. I closed my eyes and felt my heart race. Did Mr. Smith seriously just read all that out loud?

I looked at the Jury first, who looked totally swayed and heartfelt. But getting my eyes to look at Salem was a hell of a lot harder. Finally, I fought the fear and turned to face him sitting a couple feet from me.

Still cuffed, his brows dipped and he looked at me with a slight gaping mouth. His actual expression was unreadable. I hated that he was so hard to read. I offered him a shrug and a nervous smile and turned away before my heart shattered into a million pieces.

"So you see," Mr. Smith carried on, like he didn't just read my love letter, "this letter shows you exactly the type of relationship Salem had with Lana. The two of them were best friends, and close enough together to take such a picture." He referenced the locket still in his hand.

"Salem loves Lana, and wants nothing but the best for her. So when he saw his closest friend being strangled by someone he was already weary of, all the anger sprouted from there, and things just got out of hand."

My eyes darted to Salem, who looked blank. Then to Dr. MacQuoid, who still sat there limp but infuriated.

I wondered if what Mr. Smith had said was true or not. Was Salem really weary of Trevor's intentions? It didn't seem like it. Before all this happened, the two were actually pretty close. It was Salem who had convinced me living with Trevor was a good idea. But maybe he was more doubtful than he had let on. Was *I* the clueless one?

"Thank you for presenting us with your last piece of evidence," Judge Morris remarked after Mr. Smith had finished. That was all he really needed to say to clear Salem's name. But would the jury feel the same? I guess this was it. We were about to find out.

After Mr. Taylor closed his argument weakly, it was time. Judge Morris turned to the Jury and her voice projected loud and clear.

"Members of the Jury, you have now heard all the evidence. Before you reach a concluding verdict, you must listen to the instructions." She cleared her throat.

"You must decide the facts based on the evidence admitted in this trial. Do not allow anything that happens outside this courtroom to affect your decision. Do not use dictionaries or other reference materials." She paused, made sure everyone was still following along, and then continued.

"I will now tell you the law that you must follow to reach your verdict. In reaching your verdict, do not guess what I think your verdict should be based on my commentary or actions. You must not let bias, sympathy, prejudice, or public opinion influence your decision. Salem Coleman is the defendant in this case. You will be deciding based on facts and evidence whether Mr. Coleman is guilty or not guilty. You must all reach the same conclusion. If this cannot be done, this case may be retried. Does the Jury understand the instructions I have given?" Asked Judge Morris.

"Yes, Your Honor," could be heard amongst the twelve people. And with that, I watched in apprehension as the Jury stood and shuffled out of the room.

Chapter 25:

It was only now that Salem had started to worry.

His hands were trembling and he tried not to make it obvious by running them through his hair. Something he rarely did.

Mostly everyone in the courtroom went to do their own things, with the Judge's knowledge of course. Two people that stayed in the courtroom however, were the Defense and the Prosecutor; or Mr. Smith and Mr. Taylor. Salem stayed behind too, and not because he wanted to. I wanted to go talk to him but knew I wasn't really allowed, so after Judge Morris instructed me to leave, I did just that.

I had no idea how long the jury would be deliberating, but I did know that it would probably take awhile. Not that I was very fond of the court stuff.

I headed into the lobby and made small talk with a couple people to kill the time. I couldn't really go anywhere, and Lars was my ride anyway. Instead, I drank some water and ate a couple snacks offered to me.

It seemed like court people were a lot more sympathetic towards the minors, because they had to assume that a minor being in a courtroom wasn't for a good reason. But most of my free time was being spent worrying about the outcome of Salem's trial. My stomach was in a knot and I could barely shovel down the granola bar in my hand.

I felt bad for Salem, and if I thought this part of the trial was boring, he had to have had it worse than me.

It had been maybe an hour or so. More than that, probably. But it sure didn't feel like it.

It was funny how some moments it felt like everything was moving in slow motion, and then others were speeding like how Salem drove Trevor's car drunkenly. That was a funny memory. Recent, but so distant now. It made me a little sad that there was a chance we'd never be able to do that again. Even if it was dangerous, and frowned upon. I'd kill to go back to that night.

I stayed in the lobby, occasionally waving to someone as they passed. No one seemed interested in sticking around though, understandably. I guess my main concern was - would Salem be put in prison? And would Trevor get away with all this because of his money?

I stopped into the bathroom and lingered in there for awhile, staring at the mirror. I looked decent; my hair wasn't too flat but it wasn't frizzy either.

My under eyes were a dark, loomy color that I'd never dealt with before, but with all the stress I'd been through these past few months I couldn't expect anything less. My eyes were more silver than blue today, and it sounded corny but I swear their color got duller based on what I felt like. And right now, the silver showed how unhappy and shaken I was.

I rubbed them to snap out of it. There was no need for me to be analyzing my appearance while my best friend was in the other room worrying whether or not he'd see the light of day again. I mean seriously, what would I do if this was the last time I saw him?

I exited the bathroom and I guess I did so at the perfect moment because suddenly a young guy, who I think was the bailiff, started approaching me.

"Ms. Garcia?" He asked me. I looked at him and nodded. "Yes, that's me." He smiled. "Your presence has been requested. Please report back to the courtroom." He walked away, and reluctantly, I followed him.

I really didn't want to go back in there, knowing how this moment was either going to make or break my heart. But I opened the doors anyway, and prepared myself for the worst.

My eyes focused on Salem and remained there till I found my seat. He wasn't returning the glance, but instead taking deep, uneven breaths while staring at the wall. He didn't blink. Not once while I looked at him.

As I watched people shuffle back into the room in groups, I got more and more nervous. I hope I'll never have to face something like this again. The tension was *killing* me.

Finally, the Jury entered the room.

I recognized a couple faces as they each took their seats. And I knew right then that it was time to face the truth, whether it be good or god awful.

"Let's see. Is everyone here? Defense?" Asked Judge Morris. Mr. Smith stood proudly to announce his presence and then sat back down.

Judge Morris nodded and continued. "Prosecution? Are you ready?" Mr. Taylor stood, just like Mr. Smith had done, and croaked, "Yes, your Honor."

"Defendant. Mr. Coleman? Please stand." And he did.

"The Jury has reached their final verdict."

After about a minute, Judge Morris spoke again. "Will the Jury foreperson please stand?" A tall, lanky man stood on cue.

"Please state your name for the court." The man cleared his throat and said, "Lewis Solomon, your Honor."

"Has the jury reached a verdict?" She asked. Lewis said, "Yes."

A document was then exchanged between Lewis Solomon and the clerk. It was then passed to Judge Morris, who reviewed it emotionless, before setting it in front of her.

This was it. I watched in agony as the clerk stood to face everyone in the room.

"The Jury has found the defendant *not guilty* in the ruling of self-defense."

I fought the tears of joy now welling in my eyes and laughed. I laughed like a crazy person, but I didn't care. I had just received the news I had been waiting for for weeks. And Salem couldn't have been any happier either.

I looked at him with blurry eyes and he looked at me. He finally made eye contact with me, and I saw him smile. That was something I didn't see very often, but now that Salem received this news I hoped to see it a lot more. He unclenched his tight jaw and let the realization take over that he was no longer going to be seen as a felon.

The relief and happiness he now wore was something I could finally read just by staring at him. They say your eyes are like a window to your soul, and I kind of believed that. Because looking at Salem's eyes, I could see everything he was feeling. And it was all bright, and happy, and contented.

But that wasn't the only thing that made me laugh like a maniac that day. Shortly after hearing the verdict, there was something else that needed to be addressed. Dr. MacQuoid.

The clerk waited for the stirred emotion in the courtroom to simmer before making the next announcement. "While Mr. Coleman was cleared of any accusations, Dr. MacQuoid was found to be a rising suspicion. Because of this, Dr. MacQuoid will be evaluated and taken into custody for separate accusations and evidence challenged by the Defense today."

Dr. MacQuoid jumped out of his wheelchair and clenched his fists in rage. Mr. Taylor attempted to sit him back down, but he shoved him out of the way.

"What? You can't do this to me! I'm a psychiatrist! Everyone knows me! You people have no idea what you're talking about!" He cried.

However, nobody paid him any attention. Not even Hudson, who might've even had a little smirk on his face as he watched his dad get dragged away by officers. "Somebody get me a better lawyer!" He roared.

Mr. Taylor tried to reason with the clerk, but the law was the law, and no money could get Dr. MacQuoid out of this mess.

It was obvious he was the killer, and letting him back into society was just about the stupidest thing you could do. He was dangerous, and he was no stranger to the human mind. He used his knowledge to manipulate people; to ruin them. And I'm not sure what he was doing to his other patients, but if you haven't already put the pieces together, I didn't have Stockholm Syndrome. I never did.

For being in a wheelchair, Trevor sure didn't act like it. He kicked and thrusted in attempts to flee from the guards, but they weren't letting him go.

"Dr. MacQuoid, you are now under investigation in suspicion of aggravated assault and murder," said one of the guards.

"What? She was the one who cheated on me!"

The room went silent and everyone turned their attention back to Trevor, still detained in the hall. He cleared his throat and failed to take back what he said. "I didn't mean it like that," he insisted. "I wasn't talking about Debbie, or any of the women -"

The guards, who now looked even more angry, proceeded to drag him away until he couldn't be heard anymore.

So while Trevor was throwing a tantrum with the guards, Judge Morris shut the doors behind him and his escorts. I admit, it was kind of bone chilling hearing his now muffled yells as he got further and further away. But what was even scarier was that look he gave me right before he was dragged out. He looked me dead in the eyes; a stare that now burned fresh into my mind. The look that said he wasn't done with me yet. It was something I'd never forget.

So that was why he killed women. He had so much resentment in his heart because of his wife, who cheated on him. And I was gonna be next.

Judge Morris paused, stood there in silence, and then pursed her lips together. "Jury, thank you for your service today. Court is adjourned."

And that was it.

All I remembered was getting out of there, more relieved and excited and overwhelmed than ever. All that court stuff I'd been stressed out about for the past few weeks was done. And Salem, who wasn't referred to as my captor anymore, could see me again. This time, without any killer therapists or matrons getting in the way.

But before I left the courtroom, there was one more thing I needed to do. For closure, I guess.

"Hudson?" The blonde canary guy stopped in his tracks and turned to meet my gaze. "Oh. Hi." He gave me a weak smile; one that wasn't very believable. "So . . . How are you?"

He craned his neck. "Well, my dad's gonna be put away now, and I just found out my mom cheated on him and was murdered as a result, so I don't really know how to feel."

Right. "I'm sorry about your dad. And your mom. But you did the right thing. For me."

He nodded. "And for my mom."

Okay, so maybe he didn't really do it for me, but regardless, I got what I wanted.

"But your friend is free now," he continued, "so tell him I'm rooting for him." His smile returned, a genuine one this time, and then he turned to leave.

"Wait!" I exclaimed. "Don't go yet. Were you the guy I saw at the pool a few months back?"

He paused in thought, and then said, "Oh yeah, I forgot about that. Sorry to cause any trouble by the way. The reason I recognized you was because I saw your picture in the news."

Well, that made sense. At least I could stop wondering about that now. "Ah. I see. But one last thing I've been meaning to ask. What's with the cool bird tattoo?"

He ran his fingers along his neck. "My canary tattoo? I got it a few years back. I kind of regret it now, because I was young and stupid. But I actually got it to get back at my dad for how he treated me. He hates tattoos."

It was a really pretty shade of yellow, and in a way it complimented his warm-toned hair. "But of all things, why a canary?" I finally asked.

"I was waiting for you to ask that," he professed. "Did you know canaries symbolize freedom? I finally felt free after leaving my dad. Now I can travel, and just wander around. I'm kind of a drifter."

Well, that explained it. The way I always somehow ran into him. He was everywhere. So he wasn't just stalking me or something. *Canary guy liked to drift.*

"Wow. I actually didn't know that. But it's real pretty. I think your tattoo looks nice."

"Yeah, you're right. It's grown on me. Anyways, I've got a train to catch. Bye, Lana."

"Bye, Hudson." And with that, the canary guy disappeared both out of the courtroom and out of my life.

Chapter 26:

So because I was a minor, I couldn't exactly do whatever I wanted. Salem was a free man now, which meant he could.

I didn't have any contact with him and had no idea what he was doing right now, because I was still staying with Lars.

But I would see him tomorrow. It had been a week since the trial and he was all I could think about. I'd see him because now that Trevor's house was under investigation, we'd be able to collect our things there. I didn't really want to go back to that house, but I did leave a couple things behind that I wanted back. And so did Salem. That was why his backpack contents were used as evidence. Because they were found by investigators searching Trevor's house.

But even the confiscated evidence would be returned to Salem if they belonged to him. Like the locket. I hoped he didn't think it was stupid, or embarrassing to wear. I wasn't sure where the locket was right now, but I hoped it was in good hands until he collected it.

The next day rolled around rather quickly, and I couldn't contain my excitement. "Is it time to go yet?" I asked Lars as I practically pranced to the kitchen. He was drinking coffee with the television on and he chuckled seeing my excitement.

"You really miss this boy, huh?" He smiled. I nodded. That couldn't be more true.

It had taken some time to finally get Lars out the door, and I guess we weren't able to go there until the people at Trevor's allowed it. When they did, I climbed into the passenger seat and let Lars do the conversating.

"You know, at first I thought the kid was up to no good all the time. Thought maybe he was just a user or ex-juvie convict or something."

"Really?" I asked.

"But now I think I know what you see in him. I mean, he got all his charges cleared with a public defender, so that's worth something."

I nodded. "Yeah. He was telling the truth the whole time."

Lars smiled. "Seems like it. Well Lana, if there's one piece of advice I can give you now, it'd be to keep him from pummeling future psychiatrists."

We then burst out laughing together in the car. Lars had his doubts initially, but it seemed like we were finally on the same page now. *And that's worth something.*

"So," he hummed, "what stuff do you need from there?"

I paused and thought about it. I couldn't really remember. But whatever I left there was still important enough for me to want back. Because in all honesty, I didn't have many things, let alone nice ones.

Speaking of nice things, my eyes darted to the bracelet still on my wrist. I hadn't taken it off since Trevor initially put it on me, and as much as the bracelet made me angry now, you couldn't deny it was nice.

When we finally got there, I leapt out of the car. I didn't look back; didn't wait for any instructions, just looked for him. When I finally saw him standing amongst other people with gloves on, I just ran towards him. Before he could even notice me, I almost tackled him to the floor in a hug.

Startled, he caught himself before falling and came to his senses. He smashed me into the hug I'd been waiting for all week.

I could feel people staring at us, but it didn't matter. We just sort of lingered there, and instantly all my worries just seemed to leave me alone.

As I was pulling out of the hug, my shirt got caught on something around his neck. My eyes focused on a little silver heart necklace now swaying gently. *The locket.*

My eyes stayed on the locket, and when he noticed what I had noticed, he laughed. "Oh, this cute thing? Someone special gave it to me for my birthday."

I blushed. "You're wearing the locket."

He smirked. "Of course I am. Why wouldn't I be?"

I didn't say anything else. Just how happy he looked to be wearing it was enough for me to realize he loved my little gift. But my thoughts were interrupted when I heard a voice behind us.

"Okay, you two. Go ahead and grab whatever is yours and head on out so we can finish everything here."

We both headed up two flights of stairs to get to the third floor. The place was a mess, I noticed. It looked ransacked. It was a little sad to see, I'll admit. But this was Trevor's house, not mine. It was never mine. I had to remember that.

We entered Hudson's old bedroom; also canary guy's bedroom, and instantly all the memories came flooding back.

I tried to keep my composure as I looked for my things. A backpack, some clothes everywhere, a couple makeup products - nothing too important. But then I recognized a plushie sitting on the messy bed and excitedly swiped it from the sheets.

"Look," I told Salem, "it's the bear you won for me." I held up the soft plush and he smiled.

"Wow. I forgot about that. Let's not forget him." I threw the bear into my backpack, making sure not to leave it behind this time. "He's safe in my bag," I sang.

And that was it. I had nothing else.

But I didn't need anything else really. I stepped outside the room, watching as Salem ruffled through his backpack and collected clothes that littered the floor. When he was finally ready, he took one last look at the room, and I did the same. I'd probably never see this room again, and I couldn't tell if that was a good or a bad thing. But for now, I concluded it was neither. I accepted this thought and headed towards the glossy stairs waiting for me.

Salem and I stopped at the front door, and then I realized he was all on his own. "Where exactly are you staying?" I asked him wearily. I was pleasantly surprised when he told me he had enough money to rent a motel not far from here.

"Are you going back to the motel? What about me?" I said.

He pressed the back of his neck and sighed nervously. "Well, I was actually waiting for *you* to tell *me* what's next." It took me a second to comprehend what he was hinting towards, but then I understood. "You want me to stay with you?"

He shoved me playfully. "Alright kid, I'm done with the hints. I want you to live with me. Because you were right about what you said in that letter. I'm not really the smartest person without you. You keep me in check."

Then he stopped and shook his head. "That sounds selfish. What I meant is I genuinely want your company. I mean, I know you're still sixteen, but you're almost seventeen, so I figured you could make your own decisions now -"

I covered his mouth before he could keep rambling and laughed. "Shut up already. Of course I want to live with you, Salem. I thought you'd never ask. So come on, what's your plan?"

Chapter 27: **EPILOGUE**

I sighed dreamily as I looked out the window of our cute little apartment. The bright lights and the cars that crowded the streets under us made me feel like I was right at home.

If it isn't obvious, a lot has happened since the trial. Can you believe it's been a year? A whole *year!*

And it's also been a whole year since I've seen Trevor.

Part of me kind of wished he didn't turn out to be a ruthless serial killer so he could've ended up adopting me. But I was way past the whole orphan thing. I had my own life now, and I was able to make my own decisions without depending on a parent.

In case you're wondering, Salem and I did choose to live together. Only we decided it was best to leave Greenwood. Not just Greenwood, but South Carolina in general. I didn't want to be anywhere near Trevor for obvious reasons, and Salem had nothing to stay for either. So we left to start a new life in New York City; the city of opportunity.

I know, right? Who would've thought I'd be a city girl?

But seriously. I loved New York City. There were so many things to do. So many people I had yet to find. But regardless of the friends I'd make, Salem was still going to remain number one.

We were happier than ever living in New York. The apartment we rented was far from extravagant, but it was everything I needed to be comfortable.

I'm seventeen now, almost eighteen. And Salem is nineteen.

Of course, I couldn't bring everything with me. I'd miss a couple people, like Lars and his wife, who were a little sad about my departure. But they understood what I went through and why I felt this was right, so they told me to enjoy myself as long as I came to visit.

I would miss Phoebe, even though I couldn't properly say goodbye; and Hudson, even though we weren't close or anything.

But I would visit Lars and Porschia. And since Hudson just seemed to appear in the background of my life spontaneously, maybe we'd somehow find each other again. Given everything that happened last year, this idea wasn't very far-fetched.

And I got my justice. Remember Trevor's downfall? It only got worse from there.

Trevor was sentenced to life in prison without parole. Apparently, there was a lot more evidence against him than Mr. Smith had presented that day. And if you haven't already guessed, Trevor MacQuoid did turn out to be the infamous Greenwood killer. Not that it was a good thing, but it still never failed to blow my mind. I lived in a murderer's mansion for months and I didn't even know it.

Debbie had an affair with another man, which drove Trevor to insanity after he found out. He killed Debbie after they divorced, and took his anger out on all women after that. Including me, apparently. Because I was supposed to be dead.

And those ID cards? They were like his trophies. I tried not to think about this bone-chilling piece of information, because seriously, it left me disturbed for weeks. But it always somehow crept up in my mind every now and again.

All the IDs were returned to the rightful families of each victim. Mine was, to no surprise, returned to me. But I destroyed it and got a new one, because no way in hell would I hold on to that flimsy piece of plastic after hearing about it's terrible history.

Knowing Trevor was locked up and far away from me made me feel peace from the whole ordeal. But that didn't stop me from occasionally thinking about the way he glared at me before being taken away. If looks could kill, he would've finished me off right there in the courtroom.

And the feeling of his cold, veiny hands pressed on my neck, slowly cutting off all my senses. I went to therapy for a couple months after Trevor's sentencing, and that helped me heal a little. But that feeling of me begging for the life I swore I didn't want made me reconsider all my thoughts.

But I was safe now. And I was happy.

Of course, we needed to find a way to pay rent somehow. We couldn't just frolic around with some cash in our pockets like we did in North Augusta. So Salem started working as a bouncer at a nightclub. If there was one good thing he could take away from almost beating Trevor to death, it was that he knew he could throw a good punch. And clearly that looked good on his resume.

And sure, he might be working at a nightclub and all, but to my delight, he quit drinking and smoking. It was crazy seeing how much self control he had to quit them all at once like that, but he surprised me more every day.

I walked into my little bedroom and fell onto my bed. There was a window with a perfect view of the city for me to adore every night. Salem always made fun of me when he saw how amazed I was at the view; but unlike him, who grew up in Rochester, this was all new to me.

I started a little collection of teddy bears, most of which Salem bought for me on special occasions. But of course my favorite was in the middle - the one he had won for me at the arcade.

"Hey kiddo," said Salem as he stood in my doorway. "I told you to stop calling me that," I grumbled. "I'm almost an adult now."

He laughed. "Regardless of how old you are, you'll always be younger than me." I scoffed in a pretend offensive manner. "I am not that young."

He raised a brow. "The way you sit by your window watching the cars go by every night makes me think otherwise." I got up from my bed and pushed him, but I guess being a bouncer now and all, he was stronger than I remembered. So he didn't budge.

And don't think I'm just some leech sitting around all day. I'm actually trying to go to college.

Salem wasn't interested in that idea for himself; he just liked his current position and the pay was decent. But he knew how much potential I had, so he fully supported me as I applied for different colleges.

Originally, I didn't know what I wanted to be when I got older. But now, after everything I'd been through, I think it was pretty obvious I was destined to be a lawyer. So I could defend people like Salem, who needed my assistance to face their normal life again. I knew I wasn't the smartest person, or the most skilled, but one thing I did know was that I could do this. And Salem was excited to hear my career proposal too.

By now, Salem was in the kitchen. I of course went to bother him because he really was the only person I had in New York City. He was pretty protective of me within the first month of moving here, always warning me of the dangers of New York and all. I never really paid attention. I was too focused on my new life as a city girl to be concerned. But after awhile, he let his guards down and trusted I knew how to take care of myself. And I did.

"So. You think this is right?" I asked him as he started making a sandwich. He blinked. "Is what right?"

"Oh, you know. Us living in the city and all." I sounded so giddy; like I already knew the answer but just wanted to hear him repeat it. "I think so. Why? Are you having second thoughts? It's already been a year."

I threw my head back and smiled. "Of course not! I love living here. I guess I just never thought we'd make it this far."

He leaned on the counter and looked at me. "Lana, if you're talking about us," he said, "then just know I love you. And I'm sorry I don't say it very often."

I had to take a second to replay what I just heard. "You mean that?"

This time he smiled at me. "Ah, kid. You think I would just take a random girl to New York City that I didn't plan on spending the rest of my life with?"

I blushed. "Well, then I love you too." He flashed the locket around his neck and then went right back to making his sandwich as if he didn't just confess his love for me. I hated how easily he could do that. Did he not realize what he was doing to my heart right now? It was totally *racing*!

But curiosity was killing me and I had to ask him something. Even though it was in the past and we didn't really like speaking about it.

"Salem?" I asked. "I'm listening."

"The time period when you ran away - and I was at Trevor's, getting 'therapy' - what exactly were you doing out there?"

He hesitated, like he didn't want to tell me. "Well - I drank a lot. And I smoked."

I nodded. "I figured. But go on."

"I think it's been long enough since it all happened, so I guess if you really want to know I'll tell you. I started experimenting with drugs."

I raised a brow. "What kind of drugs?"

"I started getting fried."

I frowned. "What?"

"Meth, Lana. I started using ice and if I didn't stop when I did I probably would've gotten an addiction. I almost overdosed."

I gasped. "Are you serious?"

He nodded. "I almost wanted to overdose on purpose. I felt like there was no point in continuing my life if I was on the run from cops.

But you know, in a way - I have to give you credit for saving my life, because if you didn't keep showing up in my mind, I would've taken even more drugs till I was dead."

I had no idea. I was too stunned to speak.

"So then," he continued, "I was about to take more drugs until I thought about you again. And how much it'd crush you if you found out I overdosed.

So I took a walk. And before I knew it, I was back at Trevor's. I don't know what I was thinking, given that Trevor wanted me gone, but shit. If I didn't somehow find you when I did, you would've been the one dead, not me."

I shuddered. Maybe I was just too innocent, or incoherent or something, but somehow I had failed to discover *all* the facts of what happened a year ago.

"So thank you, Lana, for saving my life and making me think twice about overdosing. I never want to go back to that time, but luckily, I don't think we'll ever have to worry about going through something like that again."

"No, Salem. *You* saved *my* life. And I don't think I can ever pay you back equally for doing what you did that day."

He winked. "I guess we'll call it even."

So, yeah. I wanted to marry him. The way he could turn something so awful into something positive never failed to amaze me. But I had the whole rest of my life to live, so what was the rush? In the meantime, my priorities were to go to college and have fun while working on my career.

And in that moment, I understood just how Hudson felt when he compared his freedom to a canary. I wouldn't go as far as to get the bird tattooed on my neck, but to each their own.

As far as the bracelet, I decided to keep it. I know it would've been nicer if it was a gift from Salem, but it was diamond encrusted. Sad memories don't scuff diamonds, so as far as I was concerned, it was staying on my wrist.

And of course, the memories it held. I know most of those memories aren't pretty, but the bracelet sure is. And remembering the day Trevor gifted it to me while I was watching TV was something I didn't want to let go of just yet.

"We still going to the party, or what?" Salem asked as he slid on a dressy coat.

"Of course we are!" I beamed. "As long as you don't do anything stupid." He smirked. "With you being around, I probably won't be able to."

We were totally going to rock a party. This was the first real party we were going to in New York City, but it certainly wouldn't be the last. So when we climbed into Salem's car, I was pumped and radiating.

But as we were on the road, the car came to a sudden halt. One that wasn't very good.

Salem frowned and got out of the car to inspect it. When he got back in, he broke the news to me. "Car broke down. This blows."

My eyes widened. "What? Does that mean we're stuck out here? And what about the party?"

He clenched and then unclenched his jaw as he formed the words, "Guess we'll have to hitchhike."

AUTHOR BIOGRAPHY

Ella Hanna

Is the
author of *From
Stockholm to
Salem*. When she
was just thirteen
years old, she
started the novel
as a project and
later realized it
was worth

finishing. Born and raised in Florida, Ella has always been an animal lover, a devoted student, and a loving big sister. Now, Ella's goals are to continue writing for the remainder of her high school career. She plans to elevate her writing, honing her skills through the completion of college. She is exploring all the possible options as to where she will apply, and plans to keep her education a priority.

Made in the USA
Columbia, SC
27 October 2022

70104977R00114